‖‖‖‖‖‖‖‖‖‖‖‖‖‖‖‖

◁ **W9-DFO-969**

"Not a real marriage. More like . . . a job."

A job? Marcy listened as Steve went on, explaining something she couldn't understand. Something about the children and his problems with housekeepers and how the solution would be to hire a wife. *Hire a wife?*

"Legally we'd really be married, Marcy. You'd be my wife—and I can afford to give you everything you want."

"I see." *Everything but love.*

"So, what do you think, Marcy?"

"I think," she said, surprised to hear herself sounding so calm, "that it's wonderful of you. Really wonderful to make such a tremendous sacrifice for those children. And I'm sure—" her voice began to tremble "—I'm sure that somewhere among your acquaintances, you will find the perfect woman. Someone who will be glad to contract such a marriage. But it will not be me!"

She ran out, slamming the door behind her, rushing to the safety of her apartment, hurrying, before the tears came.

Eva Rutland, American author, lives in California, where she and her husband, retired from the U.S. government, are active in community affairs. She began writing seriously while her four children were growing up. Her articles in top women's magazines were developed into a book, *The Trouble with Being a Mama*. Since then she has had an inspirational romance published, written a musical comedy and had some skits produced on radio and television. Readers will enjoy the warmth, humor and sensitivity in the writing of this new author in the Harlequin Romance series.

To Love Them All

Eva Rutland

Harlequin Books

TORONTO • NEW YORK • LONDON
AMSTERDAM • PARIS • SYDNEY • HAMBURG
STOCKHOLM • ATHENS • TOKYO • MILAN

ISBN 0-373-02897-0

Harlequin Romance first edition March 1988

Copyright © 1988 by Eva Rutland.
Philippine copyright 1988. Australian copyright 1988.
All rights reserved. Except for use in any review, the reproduction or utilization
of this work in whole or in part in any form by any electronic, mechanical
or other means, now known or hereafter invented, including xerography,
photocopying and recording, or in any information storage or retrieval system,
is forbidden without the permission of the publisher, Harlequin Enterprises
Limited, 225 Duncan Mill Road, Don Mills, Ontario, Canada M3B 3K9. All the
characters in this book have no existence outside the imagination of the
author and have no relation whatsoever to anyone bearing the same name
or names. They are not even distantly inspired by any individual known
or unknown to the author, and all incidents are pure invention.

The Harlequin trademarks, consisting of the words HARLEQUIN ROMANCE
and the portrayal of a Harlequin, are trademarks of Harlequin Enterprises
Limited; the portrayal of a Harlequin is registered in the United States Patent
and Trademark Office and in the Canada Trade Marks Office.

Printed in U.S.A.

CHAPTER ONE

MARCY HELD THE PHONE a little distance away. Still the harsh voice boomed in her ear and thundered over the crackling wire.

"Three weeks ago! It happened three weeks ago and you're just telling me now?"

"I'm sorry, Mr. Prescott. But it was difficult to—"

His tirade cut her off. "Surely I should've been informed before now. My own sister..." He raged on, bitter, accusing. She shouldn't have been surprised. Diane had said he was explosive. For a moment, the thought of Diane shut out the voice.

Diane. Happy, laughing Diane and David. Dead.

"What the hell is going on out there in California that it takes three weeks to get a simple message to a man!" The storm of his fury swept across the miles, lashing out at her and shocking her into retaliation.

"Really, Mr. Prescott, you're acting like—" She stopped, gained control of herself. "We're wasting time. There's been enough delay as it is." She remembered the long telephone trail through faraway unfamiliar places. Ecuador, Bolivia, Colombia. Finally, in a remote corner of Peru, some distance from Cuzco, a crisp impersonal voice had informed her that Mr. Prescott was out in the field, but could be reached by radio. Was there a message?

No. No message. Marcy had left her number, explaining that it was urgent Mr. Prescott return her call as quickly as possible....

"Do you know how hard you are to reach? We've been trying to find you for days, and—"

"Well, you should have tried harder!" He was shouting now and Marcy shouted back.

"You're being unreasonable!"

"Unreasonable! For God's sake! You're telling me that my sister drowned three weeks ago and you expect me to be...be..." He broke off with a choking sound and Marcy was instantly contrite. Of course he'd be upset, hearing it for the first time.

"I'm so sorry," she said. "And I'm sorry to have to tell you like this. I apologize for the delay, but it really has been difficult to reach you."

"I see. I see. Look, I didn't mean to be rude. I—I just—"

"I understand. I know this has been a shock. I wish—"

"Are you sure? Both of them?" He spoke so quietly now that she had to strain to hear him. "How did it happen?"

As briefly as she could, she told him about the boating accident on the Sacramento River and the rescue attempts that had failed. Her own tears started again, and she was glad her office door was closed. How many times had she been told, "Marcy, try to be more professional. Don't get personally involved."? But how could she be impersonal about the Nelsons? They were like family. The same week Marcy had moved into her condominium, the Nelsons had moved into the one next door—almost two years ago. Marcy had just been transferred from the Los Angeles office, and the Nelsons, Diane said, had decided that Auburn was the perfect town for them. Small and quiet, a good place for the children to grow up and for David to write his detective novels. Marcy had become close to the family, and now she felt as bereft as Diane's brother did.

"I should have been there." He sounded lost and kept repeating the same thing. "I should have been there." Was he regretting his six-year absence?

She found herself trying to comfort him. "These things happen. There is nothing you could have done." She hesitated. He hadn't mentioned the children. "Our concern now must be for the children."

"Children?" He sounded surprised, as if he had forgotten they existed.

"Davey and little Ginger." A sob caught in her throat and she needed a minute to steady her voice. "Some...some decision has to be made."

"Oh." Now it hit him. "My God! The kids! They must be... Are they all right?"

"They're being well cared for. We—"

"Where are they? Are they with you?"

"No." She'd wanted to keep them, but it wasn't allowed. "We've placed them temporarily with Mr. and Mrs.—"

"We?"

"Placer County Child Welfare." At his startled exclamation, she hastened on. "We were given jurisdiction until we could locate you—or some other relative. *Is* there someone else we should contact?"

"No."

"You are the only living relative?"

"Yes."

"Then in that case..." She hesitated. So much to burden him with, all at once. But she had to ask. "Do you wish...that is, are you willing to assume responsibility for these children?"

"Of course." His answer was firm and that in itself made her apprehensive. He hadn't even had a chance to think it over yet. Surely he wouldn't want the responsibility of two young children, especially if he knew there was an alternative....

"I'll be there as soon as I can get a plane out. Where do I pick them up?"

Pick them up? Did he think he could just walk in and pick them up as if they were a package waiting at the post office?

"Mr. Prescott, there are certain procedures."

"Procedures?"

"Papers to be filled out. Steps to be taken to establish legal guardianship."

"I see. Have the papers ready, would you? I should be there within the next few days. Now, where will I find the children?"

"Contact me at this office when you get into town." She gave him the address. "I'm Marcy Wilson, in Placement."

"Thank you, Miss Wilson. I'll be in touch."

Marcy hung up, but her hand remained on the phone, one polished nail beating a rapid tattoo against it. She was more than a little perturbed, and it was some time before she picked up a pencil to make a notation on the pad in front of her.

September 18. Contacted by Stephen Prescott, natural brother of deceased mother. Only living relative. Indicates willingness to assume resp...

She stopped writing. He didn't *really* want the children, did he? He had never seen them. And how could he take care of them, moving about as he obviously did? She thought of his quick answer. "Of course.... Where do I pick them up?" But that was a spur-of-the-moment decision— the shock of hearing about his sister's death. He probably felt a sense of obligation.

Ha! From what she'd heard of Stephen Prescott, he wouldn't feel obliged to do anything. If she had an alternative plan—one that was actually better for the children— surely he would not object.

Marcy scratched out the last sentence and wrote instead, *Indicates that he will arrive in a few days to discuss legal guardianship.*

There! It wasn't exactly a lie. Prescott would have to be evaluated before he could obtain custody and... Marcy paused in her reflections. Next of kin had priority. If he were willing and financially capable...

That check! They might never have known of his existence if it hadn't been for that check. Marcy sat upright in her chair, vividly recalling the day Diane had shown it to her.

It had been one of those late-summer evenings, still light out, and still warm. Diane and Marcy were sitting on Diane's patio sharing cheese and wine, and watching the children at play on the lawn below them. Marcy remembered the check because the amount had been so inconceivable.

"Five thousand dollars for your birthday?"

"That's my big brother. Always willing to give me anything—except himself!" Diane's laugh held a tinge of bitterness. "I think he expects Dave to dump me at any minute. So he tries to keep me fortified with these little handouts."

"Some handout!" Marcy sputtered.

"Yes. Steve was always generous with money, even when he didn't have much to give. Once he gave me the money for a red coat." Marcy watched Diane's face take on a dreamy expression as she explained that there hadn't been much money when she and Steve were young. Their mother had died when she was two, and their father, a traveling salesman, had to spend much of the little he earned paying for their care. "It was September, and school was about to start. I was twelve—you know how clothes-conscious girls are at that age. I'd seen this red coat and I wanted it with a passion. Steve was fifteen. He'd been caddying all summer at the golf course and was saving to buy a car. He gave me the money for that coat."

Diane's voice faded, and for a moment, there was only the clatter of David's typewriter inside and the cries of the children below.

"He sounds like a good brother," Marcy ventured, feeling a little anxious as she watched Diane's eyes fill with tears.

"The very next day, he left home. Just walked out. I couldn't find him anywhere. Dad...nobody could. And...oh, Marcy, you don't know. You can't imagine what it was like." She choked on a sob. "I never knew my mother, and Dad was away all the time. And he kept changing baby-sitters. Steve was all I had, Marcy. And when he left... I hated that red coat. I had to wear it for two winters and I hated it every single minute of that time. I hated Steve, too."

"But this check... You must have seen him again—"

"Ten years later. Oh, after about two years, I guess, the postcards began. And after a while, money and presents. Every now and then he'd telephone. Always from a different place. Then, when Dad died, Steve came back. Suggested I go live with him."

"And did you?"

Diane shook her head. "I didn't need Steve then. I had Dave. And would you believe it?" Diane put down her wineglass and looked earnestly at Marcy. "I hadn't seen my brother in ten years. And we had our biggest—no, erase that. Our only fight—but it was a big one. Just because I said I was going to marry Dave. Would you believe it?"

"He didn't like Dave?"

"He didn't even know Dave. He said it was stupid to tie myself down to some jerk who'd probably walk out on me within six months. I told him he'd know all about that—leaving was something he'd been doing himself for years." Diane took a swallow of wine and sighed. "Steve looked stunned at that, and I suppose he was a little hurt. He kept telling me I was too young, that I didn't understand. But I was too mad to listen to anything he had to say. We just kept sniping at each other until he finally yelled, 'Go ahead—marry him! Get your heart broken! Ruin your life! Have a couple of kids and really mess things up!'''

"Well, I told him I hoped he'd never marry because I'd really feel sorry for his wife and kids. He said I'd never have to worry about that because he sure as hell wasn't going to."

Marcy stared at Diane. Her brother sounded completely irrational.

"I should think he would have been glad for you." Marcy thought of her sister, Jennifer. Everything had seemed so right when Jennifer and Al got married. And Marcy had been genuinely pleased for her. But in their last telephone conversation, Jennifer had sounded listless...almost unhappy.

"Well, he wasn't glad for me," Diane went on. "But later he did calm down and apologize. And I suppose we made it up. At least we got back to the postcard-and-check routine. As you can see, he's very generous." Diane held up the check. "But I haven't seen him in six years. And you know something, Marcy? I still miss him." Her eyes misted again. "I really miss the brother I had before...before the red coat."

Now, sitting alone in her office, Marcy remembered the loneliness in Diane's voice, the hunger for the brother who hadn't been there for her. Except with money. But money wasn't enough. She thought of Davey and Ginger, who, more than anything now, needed love and total commitment—a need she was sure Stephen Prescott couldn't fill.

If only I'd been home the day of the accident, Marcy thought, as she put down her pencil. But she knew it wouldn't have made any difference. Since she wasn't a relative, the sheriff would not have released the children to her.

Anyway, she hadn't been home. She'd been in Reno with Tom Jenkins for the opening of the new show at the MGM. She'd got home long after midnight. It wasn't until the next morning that she heard about the accident from a neighbor. How an officer from the highway patrol had come with the dreadful news and had tried to find someone in charge. Kim, the teenage baby-sitter, had been frightened and at a loss. Other neighbors were just as helpless. The officer had called Protective Services to pick up the children and padlocked the Nelsons' condo.

Immediately after hearing the news, Marcy had rushed to the office to confront Jo Stanford, her supervisor and close friend.

"Sit down and get control of yourself," Jo ordered, bringing her a glass of water. Marcy was crying hysterically, and it was some time before she'd calmed down enough for Jo to reason with her. "You know I can't let you have them, Marcy. I realize that you're a friend and that you've often looked after them—yes, even overnight when their parents were away. But you know this is different. You're not a relative...."

"Then if I can't have them, I want the case."

"I can't do that, either," said Jo, who ran her department as efficiently as she did her two rough-and-tumble boys. "You're too close."

"For goodness sake, Jo! These kids have just lost both their parents. They need *me*—not a stranger. I've got to see them through this. I have to, Jo."

"All right," Jo conceded reluctantly, "I'm short-staffed this week, anyway. And it's just a matter of locating the next of kin."

Later that morning, Marcy had gone to see the children. They'd been placed with Sarah and Henry Jones, a warm, loving couple who at the time had only two other children in foster care, a small baby and a boy, Troy, about Davey's age. When Marcy arrived at the house, Ginger ran straight into her arms.

"Marcy, where's my mommy?"

Marcy held her close and glanced at Davey, who was sitting quietly. Too quietly. Her heart ached for both of them.

She took them to the park, and there, by the duck pond, she tried to explain. She told them that Mommy and Daddy had gone to a place called heaven, where all good people go.

She found it very painful. Davey said nothing, but the faraway look in his sensitive dark eyes made him seem much older than his five years. Ginger, who was not quite three, started to cry. She didn't want her mommy to go anywhere, she whimpered. Who would take care of her?

Marcy's heart almost broke when Davey said, "Don't cry, Ginger. I'm going to take care of you." It was the first time he'd spoken.

Marcy wrapped her arms protectively around both children, assuring them over and over that everything was going to be all right. But was it? She thought of Diane's absent brother. Would he really want them? And if he did, would it be the best arrangement for the children? Anyway, the first procedure was to find him.

Marcy and a lawyer from the department searched through the Nelsons' papers. It was hard for Marcy to enter that familiar apartment, so reminiscent of life. And now, of death. The fuzzy bear they'd won at the county fair, just a few weeks earlier, stared at her from one corner of the beige sofa. Davey's train lay on the living-room floor, and the bowl of roses on the coffee table gave off a sweet musty scent that permeated the whole room. Marcy wanted to tidy up, smooth the rumpled beds, throw out the dead roses. But they were to touch nothing except papers that might yield information about the next of kin.

Most of the letters were from David's agent in New York. When they called him, he confirmed what Diane had already told Marcy. David had grown up in an orphanage, and had no family. All the agent could supply was David's social security number and his listed next of kin—Diane, his wife.

Marcy kept insisting that Diane had a brother. She had seen the check. Finally they found a postcard from him, mailed from Hong Kong. No address. Then they found a short note on letterhead of the Semco Oil Company, based in New York. They called the office and spoke to Stephen Prescott's secretary, who informed them that he was somewhere in South America.

So the calls began.

Meanwhile, Marcy spent as much time as she could with the children. Just loving them, trying to bring happiness back into their faces. She often took them on little excursions and was delighted when people thought they were her own.

"Because they look so much like you—at least Ginger does," Jo Stanford said. "She's got your dimples and the same wide blue-green eyes. Different coloring, though."

That was true. Ginger's curls, which tumbled freely to her shoulders, were definitely blond, while Marcy's short stylishly cut hair was the color of burnt copper.

"She's delicate and small-boned, too—like you," said Jo. "And that frail look is probably just as deceptive. I bet she's as stubborn as you are."

"I am not stubborn," Marcy protested. But she had been unaccountably pleased by the comparison. She'd always been close to these children. And now, with their parents gone, she began to wish that they could really be hers. It might just be possible, she thought, and even mentioned the idea to Jo, who looked astounded.

"You're absolutely crazy, Marcy. They're not up for adoption."

"I know. But suppose their uncle doesn't want them. Don't look at me like that. From what Diane told me about him, he—"

"Marcy, I know what you think of this uncle. But we're taking it one step at a time. He *is* the next of kin, and..." She held up a conciliatory hand. "When we get in touch with him, we'll talk about willingness and suitability. Until then..." Jo paused to look hard at Marcy. "Let's be realistic. You know the agency frowns on single-parent adoptions. Besides, how could you afford two children? You can hardly afford yourself.'' She didn't say it unkindly, but they both knew it was a reference not only to Marcy's modest salary, but to her extravagance. Twice during the past six months she'd had to ask for a salary advance.

''Why don't you get married and have your own children?'' Jo suggested. ''There's Gerald.... No. Not Gerald. But there's that banker, Tom Jenkins. Now, he could afford you. Let's see, I think Jenkins is your best bet. Why don't you go after him?''

Marcy just smiled. She didn't tell Jo that Tom was already hinting at marriage, and that she was having a hard time fending him off. She'd always been fond of Tom, but she didn't feel special about him—or about anyone else for that matter. And she certainly couldn't get married just to take care of Ginger and Davey!

Then she thought of Jennifer. Her sister, who lived in nearby Shingle Springs, was married and financially comfortable and had recently said she wanted to adopt a child. Marcy was sure she'd be happy to have Ginger and Davey. The children would be family then....

The moment Jo went back to her own office, Marcy called Jennifer. But her sister no longer seemed as enthusiastic as she'd been when they had previously discussed adoption. Marcy hung up the phone with the same sense of vague uneasiness she'd felt after their past few conversations. It wasn't like Jennifer to be so evasive, so...so apathetic. Why had she changed her mind? Was something wrong? Marcy vowed to visit her sister and find out. Soon.

After that, she had resolved to follow Jo's advice. To take things one step at a time. She knew she'd been very unprofessional about this case. And that was exactly what Ginger and Davey had become, she reminded herself—another one of her cases. She would just have to wait until she heard from Stephen Prescott.

And now she had. Marcy picked up the folder and got to her feet, still deep in thought. He'd said he would come. To take the children?

There was a light tap at her door, and without waiting for an answer, Gerald Sims walked in. He was robust and sandy-haired, with a sprinkle of freckles across his nose. He wore a brown tweed suit and his thank-goodness-it's-Friday smile.

"Day's end. Let's hit the road, toad!"

Marcy repressed a wince and made herself return his smile.

"How about dinner in Folsom?" Gerald asked. "The Gaslight's got a new show going. I hear it's pretty good."

"Sorry, Gerald. Not tonight. I promised to take the Nelson kids—"

"Again!"

Marcy just nodded. She went into the larger office and placed the folder in Anita's basket, which was already overflowing.

"All work and no play—that's Dullsville, kid."

"It's not dull. We're going to the circus. Would you like to come along?"

"No, thank you." Gerald walked her to the car, declaring that after working with kids all week, he'd had enough of them. He meant to enjoy his weekend—in adult company.

Marcy wondered about his remarks as she drove home. If Gerald didn't really like children, why hadn't he transferred to another department? Marcy loved them and if she had her way... Well, she wouldn't think about that now.

She turned into the Woodside complex and parked her Volkswagen. Living in a Woodside condo, with a fireplace and a loft bedroom, was one of her extravagances. The apartment buildings, which had been designed to take advantage of their natural setting, were surrounded by the massive trees of the Auburn woods. Now the landscape was aglow with red, green and gold beauty, as the late-afternoon sun glistened on the colorful leaves of early autumn.

Marcy's feet crunched along the gravel path, and she scooped up a handful of walnuts before climbing the steps to her apartment door. She'd have to hurry and change; she still had to stop by her bank's automatic teller before she picked up the children. She tried to figure out how much money she would need. Three tickets—no, four. On impulse, she'd also invited Troy, the other boy in the home; he got out so seldom. Okay then, for the tickets and other extras—would forty dollars do it? Would that leave enough for her car payment and the rest of the month? Oh well, she'd think about that tomorrow.

MONDAY AND TUESDAY were hectic. The Braxton boy wasn't working out with the Emorys and might have to be moved again. Poor little ten-year-old. Too many problems. Too many parents. She made an appointment to discuss the case with Dr. Jackson; perhaps they could arrange for counseling. Tuesday afternoon, two abused children were brought in and had to be placed immediately. The cases piled one on top of the other, and Marcy found herself working late, after Jo and everyone else had already left.

She went into the central office for the Braxton boy's file so she could take it to her six o'clock meeting with Dr. Jackson. But the folder wasn't in the filing cabinet nor in Anita's basket. Someone should speak to her about the filing, Marcy thought irritably. Then she noticed a stack of folders on top of the cabinet. Perhaps... Yes, there it was, right in the middle. She tried to ease it out.

"Excuse me, please."

Marcy jumped, jerked the folder, and the whole pile came tumbling down, scattering folders and papers over the floor.

That did it! The perfect disastrous end for a perfectly disastrous day! Exasperated, she turned to face the intruder.

"My fault! Sorry." The man had bent down toward the fallen papers.

"No! Don't touch those!"

At her sharp cry, he straightened, suddenly towering over her. He had black hair and very dark eyes, she noticed, and a face so deeply tanned, so vibrantly alive, that it was as if he'd brought the whole outdoors in with him. He gestured toward the papers.

"I'd like to help, but..."

Marcy caught the hint of puzzled amusement and felt flustered. "It—it's just that they have to be sorted," she explained, "and they're...well...confidential."

"Oh. Okay, in that case, I won't look." He flashed her a warm, conspiratorial smile. Then he bent down again, resting easily on his heels, like an athlete. "I'll pick them up and you can sort."

Mechanically, Marcy sank to her knees to replace the papers he handed her. Brown...Jones...Johnson... No, that went in the Thomas file. The names floated before her, and she felt clumsy and confused.

Darn Anita and her stupid filing! Then Marcy flushed. She knew it wasn't the scattered folders that had disconcerted her. It was something about his smile, a smile that made her feel strangely excited and a little giddy. The way that lock of hair kept falling across his forehead reminded her of...someone. Who was he? Could he be the new lawyer they were expecting? He looked so...outdoorsy. Even in that well-cut business suit. His hands looked so brown against the papers...strong and work-roughened. Not the hands of a man who sat behind a desk all day.

Marcy finally put the folders back on the filing cabinet, hoping everything was in order. She turned to him, a little breathless.

"Thank you. Now, how can I help you?"

He fumbled in his pocket and produced a piece of paper. "I'm looking for Placement."

"You're in the right office." Maybe he *was* the new law-yer, she thought hopefully.

"Good." The smile reappeared, and she watched, fasci-nated by the way his eyes lit up and crinkled at the corners. "I'm to see a Marcy Wilson."

"I'm Marcy Wilson."

He held out his hand. "Steve Prescott. I'm here to pick up the Nelson children."

CHAPTER TWO

FOR A MOMENT, Marcy could only stare. This was Stephen Prescott? She had expected...what? Well, certainly not this handsome sun-bronzed man with such friendly good-humored eyes that...Davey! Davey's eyes! No wonder he looked familiar.

"Miss Wilson—it is *Miss*? I want to thank you. I really appreciated your call, and I came as soon as I could. Now, I'll need some directions. Where do I pick up the children?"

Marcy pulled herself out of her daze.

"You can't!" She caught herself and gave him an apologetic smile. "That is, not just yet. But I'm glad you're here, Mr. Prescott. We've been waiting for you to arrive. Won't you come this way, please, and we can talk."

She led the way into her office, the high heels of her tiny boots clicking on the hardwood floor. His footsteps echoed behind hers, and she was ridiculously glad that she had worn her black boots with the stylish ankle cuffs. Glad that her black gabardine skirt made her look trim and smart—then was annoyed with herself. Why on earth should she care how she appeared to Stephen Prescott? And what was making her feel so flustered? She took several deep breaths and was almost composed by the time she reached her desk. He sat down when she gestured toward a chair, but Marcy was acutely aware of his steady gaze, even as she lifted the wide cuff of her turquoise silk blouse to glance at her watch.

Almost six.

"I'll be with you in a moment," she said. "I just have to make one quick call." She dialed Dr. Jackson's extension and informed his secretary that she had an emergency. Would it be convenient to see him in the morning instead?

"Thank you," she finished, then turned to the man in front of her. "You got here in good time."

"Yes," he answered. "I arrived in Sacramento this afternoon, and rented a car. There was no connecting flight."

"No. We're rather isolated here in Auburn," she said automatically, her mind racing, trying to focus on the real issue. Ginger and Davey. Their future, their happiness. With this man? Marcy tried to brace herself against the strange effect he was having on her. She remembered what Diane had said: *I really miss the brother I had before the red coat.* Diane... "I'm extremely sorry about your sister and her husband. I know this is very difficult for you."

"Thank you." He shifted in his chair. "More difficult for the kids, I think. That's why I came right away."

"How long do you plan to stay?"

"Let's see. I have a meeting in New York the day after tomorrow...."

Marcy felt herself grow hot. He really did think he could just barge in and snatch up the kids!

"That doesn't give us much time," she said, more curtly than she'd intended.

"Well, I'll be here all day tomorrow. I do have to see a Sheriff Olsey, though. He sent me a cable."

"May I see it?"

"The cable?"

"Yes. And perhaps a passport or driver's license." He frowned and she opened her hands in a gesture that was helpless as well as explanatory. "Agency regulations. I don't doubt that you are who you say you are, but I'm required to have positive proof before I can proceed."

"Of course." He handed her the crumpled cable and a worn driver's license, an international one that had been issued in England.

"You live in England?" she asked, noting the license number on a pad and wondering if that was where he planned to take the children.

"No. I—er..." He started to add something but changed his mind. "Satisfied?" he asked, when she handed the identifying articles back to him.

"Yes."

"So it's okay for me to get the kids?"

She looked again at her watch.

"It's rather late. Perhaps—"

"Yes, I know it's late, but I don't have much time. Look..." He stood up abruptly, running a distracted hand through his hair. His voice was heavy with impatience. "Look, Miss Wilson. It was already three weeks after the accident when you contacted me. But when you called and asked me to come and pick up the kids—"

"I did not ask you to come and pick up the kids."

He stared at her. "You certainly did. You told me—"

"I asked if you were willing to assume responsibility."

"Same thing."

"Not quite." Marcy folded her hands and looked up at him, forcing herself to speak calmly. "If you remember, when we talked on the phone I told you that there were certain procedures."

"So give me the papers. I'll sign them."

She shook her head. "It's not quite that simple." She paused. This was not the time to discuss references or proof of stability. "Mr. Prescott, it's late. Ordinarily, this office would have been closed by the time you arrived."

"I'm sorry." There was that smile again, touching some chord inside her that leaped in response. "I do appreciate your taking this time. It's just that I'm anxious about the kids. I don't want them to think they're abandoned."

"The children are being well cared for. Mr. and Mrs. Jones are warm, experienced foster parents and they've been wonderful for Ginger and Davey."

"Well, okay. Yes. But..." He was no longer smiling, and Marcy noticed that his face looked strained and anxious. "Couldn't I... Look, I want them to know that I'm here for them, that they don't have to live with strangers."

How ironic, Marcy thought. Who was more of a stranger than he?

"I understand. I know how anxious you are to see them." She hesitated. "I gather you've never met the children."

"Well, no." He shook his head. "You see, I travel quite a bit and—"

"Then perhaps it would be best if you give them a chance to get acquainted with you first. If you like, I could take you out there in the morning and introduce you." Again she hesitated. "They've known me for some time. I live next door to their place and I became very close to the family."

He looked at her with new interest.

"You knew them? Diane?" She nodded and he leaned forward. "You've been with them? Talked? Were you there that Sunday?"

"No. But later."

"Tell me." He sat back in his chair, as if he were suddenly very tired, and regarded her earnestly.

So she had to tell it again. More detailed this time—how the river was dragged, though the bodies weren't recovered. How they'd placed the children. How they'd searched the apartment for clues to his whereabouts. When she finished, he sat quietly, a faraway look in his eyes. Like Davey.

"Did you get settled? Find a hotel room?" she asked gently.

He came to with a start. "Yes. The Auburn Inn."

"Then you could meet me here tomorrow. At ten?" Then she remembered her appointment at nine with Dr. Jackson.

"No. Perhaps we should say ten-thirty. We could go out to see the children."

"Yes. All right." He was still not looking at her and he sounded a little subdued.

"Then we can come back here and discuss legal guardianship."

"Legal guardianship? Discuss it? What are you talking about?" Now he looked directly at her, his eyes wary and alert. She could have kicked herself.

"The procedure I mentioned." She kept her tone light, and stood up, her signal that the conference was over. "We'll talk about it tomorrow."

He, too, stood. "Wait a minute. You keep talking about this procedure. What do you mean, 'legal guardianship'?"

Oh, Lord! she thought. Now I've got his hackles up. Establishing legal guardianship was such a routine procedure for agency employees that they tended to forget it wasn't something lay people ever thought about. Well, he ought to be forewarned. It was only fair to explain.

"You see, Mr. Prescott, because of the very tragic circumstances—with no will and no relative to take charge—the children were made wards of the court. Just temporarily," she added hurriedly, as she saw his brow crease. "It's a legal requirement. Their case has been assigned to me."

"Case?"

She nodded. "It's fairly routine. But before you can be granted custody, you have to satisfy the court that—"

"Look, lady, don't give me all that legal hogwash." He leaned across the desk, a dangerous glint in his eyes. "We're talking about my sister's children. God knows, I wish she were here to take care of them herself. But she isn't. So I'm taking them! And I don't intend to let a lot of red tape stop me!"

"We're not here to stop you. In fact . . ." She swallowed. "I'm here to help you. But you may wish to secure the services of an attorney."

"What the hell do I need with an attorney?" He threw up his hands in exasperation. "Look, you know I'm the kids' uncle. You sent for me yourself and—"

"You're absolutely right, Mr. Prescott. You do have priority," she said, hoping to placate him. "But, in the absence of a will, the law is for your protection as well as for the children's."

He seemed calmer but still looked dubious. Marcy spread her hands.

"I just wanted you to know that you have the option of retaining an attorney. But it's not necessary. I'm very familiar with the procedures. And, as I said, I'm here to help you work things out." She smiled, but he did not smile back. "Now, it really is late and all this will take some time. So I'll see you here tomorrow at ten-thirty."

He shrugged, as if acceding to the note of dismissal in her voice.

"Okay. Ten-thirty."

When the door closed behind him, Marcy sank back in her chair, engrossed in thought. She'd told Steve Prescott she was there to help him.

But that wasn't quite true. Because helping Steve Prescott was the last thing on her mind. She had been deep in plans for Ginger and Davey, plans that definitely excluded their uncle.

The door opened, and she looked up to see him again.

"I wanted to ask you something."

"Yes?"

"Diane. You said you were her friend. Do you know... Could you tell me..." His face was sober and very intent. "Was Diane happy?"

"Very happy," she said. "I've never known a happier family."

"I'm glad," he said simply, and she sensed the relief in his voice. "Thank you, Miss Wilson." Then he was gone.

Marcy sat staring at the closed door. He cared! He really did care about Diane. Even if he hadn't seen her for six years. Maybe he cared about the children, too. But was caring enough? If he was going to be away for weeks at a stretch...

One step at a time, she reminded herself. When the children met him the next day, she would watch their reaction. She'd watch his just as carefully. As when he filled out the evaluation papers, she'd find out a lot more about him.

I can be professional. I can be fair. And I will do what is best.

SHE DECIDED to treat herself to dinner at Sutton's that night. Cooking was not a favorite pastime, especially when it was just for herself. She usually ate at Sutton's once or twice a week. On weekends it was always crowded with tourists, but weekdays were quiet, and the food was consistently good.

On the way in, she met Gerald Sims. Marcy liked Gerald in spite of his silly rhymes. *Hit the road, toad,* indeed. But he was fun and they shared an easy, bantering friendship.

His broad face broke into a grin when he saw her. "Well, well, here's little Marcy Sunshine herself. Tonight's my lucky night. How about sharing a Chateaubriand?"

"Only if we go dutch," she said. Gerald's salary was no larger than her own, and he was supporting an ailing father.

"No argument from me on that score, kid. My bankroll's on the skids."

Laughing together, they entered the big dining room with the high-beamed oak ceilings and the roaring circular fireplace. That was another reason Marcy liked Sutton's—the cozy, homey atmosphere.

Ma Sutton greeted them, and Gerald joked with her as she led them to their table. Glancing across the room, Marcy was surprised to see Stephen Prescott. He was seated at a table by the window.

"That's the Nelson children's uncle," she told Gerald. "He arrived this afternoon."

"Good. That means you'll have more time for me."

Marcy wasn't listening. She was staring at Prescott. He hadn't been served yet, and was gazing out the window. He looked forlorn, even a little bewildered. Marcy felt a tug of guilt. She realized that she hadn't considered his position at all. Here was a man who had just lost his only sister, whom he had obviously loved. She remembered the way he'd asked, *"was Diane happy?"*

And now he was about to have two small children thrust upon him. He was obviously unequipped to look after them, yet he hadn't hesitated. "I'll be there," he'd promised. "I'll pick them up." And he'd been as good as his word.

Impulsively Marcy stood up. "Come on, Gerald. I think we should ask Mr. Prescott to join us."

The surprised Gerald followed her to Prescott's table. He rose to his feet at their approach.

"Hello, again," Marcy said. "I'd like you to meet my friend, Gerald Sims. Gerald, Stephen Prescott." The two men shook hands and exchanged greetings.

"I see you haven't been served yet. Why don't you join us?" Marcy urged.

He looked at Gerald. "I don't like to intrude."

"You won't be intruding. Anyway, it's no fun to eat alone."

Gerald seconded her invitation, and soon the three of them were seated together. The conversation was rather stilted at first. Gerald mentioned the boating accident and offered his condolences. Marcy, seeing the look of sadness on Prescott's face, felt compelled to change the subject.

"We found Mr. Prescott in South America—in Peru, as a matter of fact."

"Oh." Gerald was immediately diverted. "What were you doing there?"

"Wildcatting."

"Huh?"

Prescott grinned. "Speculating for oil. We do some soil testing, maybe a little sporadic drilling."

"In South America?"

"Everywhere. Anywhere. I was in Saudi Arabia last week." He said it so casually, a man accustomed to traveling swiftly from one end of the earth to the other. How, Marcy wondered, could two small children fit into this type of life?

"That must be exciting," she heard Gerald say.

"I guess." Prescott looked up to smile at the waitress, who was setting a plate of salad before him. The woman positively beamed in response.

Foolish girl. He bestows that smile on everyone—like sunshine. Appalled at herself, Marcy dug into her own salad, trying to block out the thought. It was of little concern to her how Stephen Prescott smiled. Or at whom. She turned her attention to the conversation.

Prescott was explaining that Semco Oil was a relatively new company, speculating in new areas. "Where the big companies have not yet dared to go," he said. "Remote places. Unsettled and untamed."

"Must be rough," Gerald commented. "Can't be easy living."

"Well, yeah, you don't find any Hiltons out there."

Or schools either, Marcy thought, her mind on the children. "But you like it?" she asked.

"Yes, I do," he admitted, as he cut into a piece of steak. "I guess I like the freedom—the space. The feeling of being unencumbered by buildings and people."

Marcy thought of her first impression—a man who brought the whole outdoors in with him.

"Don't think I'd like it," Gerald was saying. "Give me lights and action."

"Oh, it has its compensations." Steve hesitated. "I guess you feel close to nature.... It's as though you've never seen a sunset until you've watched the sun go down behind the Andes, all red and gold and purple. Beautiful." He broke off, looking a little sheepish. "Yeah, I like it," he said with a slight laugh, "except for the snakes."

"Snakes!" Marcy almost choked on her wine.

"Yeah." He gestured with his fork. "Do you know, one morning last week I started to put on my boot and darned if there wasn't a purple viper crawling out of it."

"Damn! What did you do?" asked Gerald.

"Do? I kicked the boot across the tent and hopped up on my bed. Acted like a fool." Marcy shuddered, surprised to see Gerald laughing.

Prescott nodded at him. "Go ahead, laugh! That's what all the guys do. They know I'm scared to death of the bloody things."

"And for good reason," Marcy said. "A lot of snakes are deadly!" Goodness, would he be taking the children where there were poisonous snakes? "Do you see many of them?"

"Snakes? Yes, I do." He leaned toward her. "Do you know there are men who've been in this business for twenty years and have never seen a snake? And I've seen nine—this year. Last month in Kenya, I picked up a pile of firewood and right on top was a puff adder." He told how he had scattered the firewood and abandoned the area.

"I can stand up to two-legged or four-legged creatures," he concluded. "But I hate snakes. You can't trust 'em...." He shook his head. "Just like women."

Just like women? The words had been muttered under his breath and Marcy couldn't be certain of what she'd heard. But it sure sounded... *Can't trust women.* Did he mean...

"Well, I think I've bored you enough." Prescott stood up. "It was kind of you to let me join you. But it's been a long day, and I think I'll turn in. Glad to have met you, Mr. Sims. Tomorrow at ten-thirty, Miss Wilson.''

"Good night.'' Marcy stared after him, trying to deal with a mixture of confused emotions. There was something about him, something appealing. A man brave enough to admit fear. *Snakes...just like women...can't trust 'em.* Was that what he'd said? She must have misunderstood. He couldn't have....

"Seems like an all-right guy.''

"Oh! Oh, yes.'' Reluctantly Marcy turned back to face Gerald.

"Eat up,'' he said. "You're only halfway through that steak.''

But for some reason, Marcy didn't feel hungry anymore.

"All taken care of,'' Ma Sutton said when they stopped at the counter to pay their bill. "That nice gentleman paid for everything.''

He *is* nice, Marcy thought. Charming. But I have to think of Ginger and Davey, of their needs. A single man—always away, often in dangerous places. Is he right for them?

CHAPTER THREE

MARCY WAS AT DR. JACKSON'S OFFICE before nine the next morning. But he didn't get there himself until nine-thirty and then had to leave immediately to be in court at ten. So she had no chance to tell him that Jimmy's hostility and belligerence were just the brittle exterior of a lonely, frightened child who...

"For Pete's sake, Marcy, the man's a psychiatrist. Don't you think he can spot a facade?" Jo shook her head. "You can't smooth all the paths, you know. Sometimes a kid has to stumble along on his own. Anyway, you'd better run along. Stephen Prescott's been waiting for an hour."

"He wasn't due until ten-thirty! I guess he didn't know I had another appointment. But I told him ten-thirty and he barges in here at nine."

"He seemed put out when I told him you weren't here. I sat him in your office."

But Stephen Prescott wasn't sitting. He was impatiently pacing the narrow confines of Marcy's office and silently berating her for not being there.

Just where was this Miss Efficiency Wilson now? She seemed mighty anxious to close the office last night. To go and meet her boyfriend. So they couldn't get anything done then. But he hadn't tried to push. Instead, he'd come in early this morning to get the legal details out of the way, so he could fetch the kids and leave. He'd postponed the New York meeting until three o'clock tomorrow. He'd be on time if he could catch that early flight out of Sacramento in the morning.

Where on earth was she? He picked up a paperweight, looked at it, set it back on the desk.

Lord, it was hot! Didn't they have any air-conditioning in this place?

He took off his jacket and threw it on the chair, then loosened his tie. He stood with his hands in his pockets, studying the pictures on the wall. A finger painting of the three bears done in black and blue. A crayon sketch of a lopsided house with smoke coming out of the chimney. An indefinable yellow blob—could it be a cat? Kid's pictures. He thought of Diane's kids and a lump rose in his throat. What did they look like? Did they draw such pictures?

Diane...I'm sorry this happened. I'm glad you were happy. I'm sorry about leaving you back then, but...Mrs. Mason liked you and I thought you'd be all right. Anyway, I had to get out of there. I had to. I know you never understood, but I'll make it up to you. I promise. The kids will never want for a thing. They won't be shoved around like we were. I promise. I'll make it up to you, Diane.

"Good morning. Are you admiring my gallery?"

Trying to swallow the lump in his throat, he turned to face Marcy's bright smile. She looked fresh and serene, and absolutely stunning in that soft, green coatdress. It made those big blue eyes look almost green. Her thick, vibrant copper hair was smooth, curling gently around her piquant, dimpling face.

He stiffened. He knew the type! Probably spent the whole morning primping. And now here she was, wasting time with small talk when he was in a hurry.

"They're originals, you know."

"What?"

"The pictures. Budding young artists whose paths have crossed mine." Gifts of love, from children she loved, Marcy thought. Why on earth was he looking at her like that? "I'm sorry to keep you waiting. But I thought you understood that I had another appointment this morning."

"No, I didn't. I got here early so we could finish up and the children and I could leave on the early plane tomorrow."

She stared at him. "That's impossible."

"Why?"

"You can't get the children today." Marcy took off her shoulder bag and placed it on the desk.

"Why not?"

She spoke in slow, careful tones, fighting to curb her impatience. "I thought I explained to you. There are certain procedures—"

"Okay, fine." He gestured toward her desk. "Will you get those papers and do whatever you have to do so I can leave?"

"I'm not stopping you from leaving today. But you can't take the children."

"Why can't I?" His glare was so menacing that Marcy felt weak.

She leaned against the desk to support herself but her voice remained firm. "I already explained to you that there are certain things that have to be done first."

"Well, do them!" He threw up his hands in exasperation. "Look, I came as soon as you phoned me. Now that I'm here, you want me to sit around for ten days or so—"

"Might I remind you that you only arrived last night— *after* office hours."

"Might I remind *you* that I've been here one full hour cooling my heels waiting for you!"

"Your appointment was for ten-thirty." She glanced at her watch. "It's just that now." He was completely impossible! How could she ever have considered him nice? "I've arranged for you to go out and visit the children and—"

"I don't want to visit the children. I want to take them with me."

Marcy gripped the edge of the desk and tried to keep her voice calm. "I thought we decided last night that we would give them a chance to know you."

"*You* decided." Impatiently he jingled the change in his pocket. "They'll get to know me. They're going to live with me."

"Maybe," she couldn't help saying.

He frowned. "What do you mean, maybe?"

She drew a deep breath. "You will have to file a petition requesting that you be named legal guardian. But first, there are some questions you have to answer, and you'll need to give us references."

"All right. But let's make sure we have one thing straight. I will get the children."

"Probably."

"No. Not probably. Certainly. I'm their only living relative. That must give me some rights."

"I don't deny that. Of course you have priority."

"Okay. So get whatever it is you want me to sign, and I'll sign it. Then I'll take the children and be out of your way."

Marcy threw up her hands.

"You may sign it, but you won't take the children today."

"We'll see about that."

"Indeed we will." Marcy stormed around her desk, jerked open a drawer and plucked out a petition form. She carefully restrained herself from slamming it down in front of him. "If you will complete this form, sir."

He gave her a sharp look before he pulled over a chair and took a pen from his jacket. On one corner of her desk he began to fill out the form. Marcy waited quietly, her hands folded.

When he'd apparently finished, she reached for a guardianship referral form, skipping down to the pertinent questions concerning the proposed guardian.

"Name?" she asked.

He looked up. "What?"

"I have to have your full name."

"Stephen Alan Prescott."

"Age?"

"Thirty-two."

"Occupation?"

"I'm in oil."

In oil?

"Please be more specific, sir."

"Vice president, Semco Oil Company."

Marcy continued the routine questions and when she came to the end, she leaned slowly back in her chair. For a moment they looked at each other; then he abruptly averted his eyes.

"Okay, here's my petition." He pushed the completed form toward her.

She picked it up, glancing at *Reason For Request*. In bold black printing he had written: "I am the only living relative. I want the children. I am willing and able to take care of them."

"Now, is that everything?" he asked, rather crossly.

"Yes, but I have to—"

"You've got the names there to check about references." He pointed to the paper. "I've put down phone numbers. Now, would you get busy calling them so they can okay me?"

"Mr. Prescott, that isn't how we do things. It takes more than a phone call. I'll be sending a questionnaire to each of these people. It has to be completely filled out and signed, then returned to us before we can make a recommendation to the judge."

He slapped a hand to his forehead. "I don't believe this. You give me the third degree. Then you have to write all over the country to confirm what I've already told you?"

"Those are the rules, Mr. Prescott. I don't make them, but I have to abide by them. It's my job."

"Rules! You can't do this; you can't do that. I don't believe you want me to have the children!" In a sudden burst of temper he stood up, shoving back his chair.

Marcy looked at him, conscious of a little tremor of guilt. Could he read her mind? Well, all right, she did have reservations about delivering Ginger and Davey into the hands of this ill-tempered man, who talked as if they were a package to be collected. But she was going strictly by the rules.

"That is not my decision to make," she said crisply.

"Well, you seem to have a hell of a lot to do with it." He ran a distracted hand through his hair. "I rush halfway across the world to see about these kids, and what happens? I'm bogged down in legal hogwash."

"I'm very sorry you feel that way, Mr. Prescott." Marcy called upon every vestige of her training to keep her voice professional. "Now, I have to clarify a few of your answers to these questions. First, a post office box is not a legal domicile."

"Oh. Well, I maintain a suite at the Waldorf, but I'm in New York so seldom, it's better to have my mail go to the post office."

"I see... Then the Waldorf is your legal residence?"

He nodded.

"How many bedrooms in your suite?" she asked.

"How many bedrooms? Why do you want to know that?"

"If this is where you're planning to take the children, we need to know whether or not the accommodation conforms to agency requirements," she said crisply. "Someone in New York must inspect the premises before you're approved."

"I don't believe this! I don't believe it!" He looked so frustrated that some of Marcy's anger dissolved. She remembered that this whole situation had been thrust on him less than a week before.

"Listen," she said. "I know this all sounds unnecessary to you, but we do have to be careful. We have to proceed slowly."

"You're right about being slow." He leaned across the desk, tapping his finger on it. "If I ran my business like you run this office, I'd stay in the hole!"

Marcy sat up straight and glared at him. "This is not a business! We deal with lives. At this particular moment we are discussing and planning for three lives."

"Three?"

"Ginger's, Davey's . . . and yours."

"Mine?" His brow creased and he gave her a puzzled look.

She nodded emphatically. "Have you considered how the care of two small children is going to affect your current life-style?"

"Don't give me that." He shook his head impatiently. "I know children!"

"Have you considered that children have to stay put? That they have to be near schools and—"

"I'll take care of all that."

"How will you take care of it?"

He looked down at her, his face tight. "That, dear lady, comes under the heading of my own concern."

"No, sir. That's my concern." Marcy gripped the pencil so hard that it broke in her hand and she stared at it in surprise. Then, gazing earnestly up at him, she struggled to organize her thoughts. She knew that as an able and willing uncle he would almost certainly receive custody. But he had to be made aware of the children's special needs and he had to prove that he could meet them. She would see to that, and thank heaven she had the rules to back her up! "Mr. Prescott, what I'm trying to explain is that the agency has to be satisfied with your arrangements for the children—where you're going to take them and who's going to look after them."

"*I'm* going to look after them! Why else would I have come here?"

"Who's going to look after them when you're in Peru?"

"Do you suppose there aren't any children in Peru?"

"Are you saying you'd take them with you?"

"I don't know."

"Well, these are the kinds of things we have to know before we can recommend custody."

"Damn it, why are we talking about Peru?" He flung up his hands and took several exasperated steps, before turning to face her again. "I don't know when I'll be back there—maybe not for years. Look, all this adds up to one thing. You're not letting me take the kids today."

"That's right."

"Couldn't I have them on a temporary basis until you get all this thrashed out?"

"No," she said forcefully. "You can visit them. But you cannot take them with you—especially not out of state."

"There must be someone else I could talk to. Don't you have a supervisor?"

"Yes. Mrs. Stanford."

"Will you kindly direct me to her? Maybe she'll listen to reason."

Without a word Marcy picked up the phone.

There was utter silence in the room while they waited.

When the supervisor at last appeared, Steve looked toward Marcy, who had swiveled her chair around to face the window, as if to divorce herself from the whole proceeding.

He turned to the woman who had come in. He felt ill at ease and strangely intimidated by the five-foot-tall lady who stared up at him through her bifocals.

"I'm Mrs. Stanford. You wanted to see me?" she asked.

"I'm Steve Prescott, the Nelson children's uncle. I've been talking with Miss Wilson," he said hesitantly. He glanced at Marcy, who still had not turned around. "And I can't seem to get anywhere with her. She chased me down and I suppose I . . . well, I'm grateful to her for that." He glanced again at the back of Marcy's chair. "But now that I'm here, she's got me involved in a lot of paperwork that I really don't have time for. I'm willing to do whatever is necessary, give you whatever you need, but I'd like to get on with it and take the children. And I'd like to do it, now, while I'm here."

"I understand how you feel, Mr. Prescott, but . . . let's sit down and go over this one step at a time." When they were seated, she looked briefly in Marcy's direction, then back at him. "Didn't Miss Wilson explain to you that there are certain procedures? That we have to check references and—"

"I gave her the names of people she can call for references, and I asked her to hurry it up, get in touch with them by phone, but she refuses. Anyway, the main reference you need is that I'm their uncle. Isn't that enough?"

"Not really. There are other considerations we have to take into account."

He stirred in his chair. "I don't understand this. I really don't. When she called me, I came immediately. I thought you'd already decided I was the logical person to take custody of the children."

He listened impatiently as the supervisor painstakingly went over the same points Marcy had already covered. He sat there, stubbornly silent, occasionally shaking his head until, finally, she sighed in frustration.

"Look, Mr. Prescott, we are legally obligated by the state of California to fulfill these requirements." She spoke in a slow, deliberate voice, enunciating every word. "It is not our choice. It is for the protection of the children."

He jumped up then, shoving back his chair. "State of California, huh? Well, there must be some way the rules can be stretched. There must be someone who can put the pressure on. I'll call my lawyer. He knows the governor."

Marcy's chair swung around suddenly and she got quickly to her feet. Both of them turned startled faces to her as she spoke.

"Mr. Prescott, I gather that you loved your sister very much."

"Yes," he answered, feeling a little stunned. "Of course I did."

"Therefore you love—are determined to love—her children."

"Yes." He was subdued now, staring wide-eyed at Marcy.

"I love them, too, Mr. Prescott. I've known them for more than two years and I love them very much." Marcy's voice broke and he was startled to see tears in her eyes. "And I will not—do you understand me?—I will *not* have them hurt anymore. I will not have them further traumatized by you!"

He was obviously taken aback, and said almost imploringly, "But I have no intention... I would never hurt them. I just want—"

"—to get the kids out of here!" Marcy snapped. "All I hear from you is *get*! 'I want to get the kids.... I want to get out of here!' Get! Get! Get! You want to get the kids and get out of here and go about your business! You want to drag them off with you to some meeting in New York and Lord knows where else after that. You don't want to disturb yourself one little bit to see that these kids have a pleasant transition."

"But I—" He started to speak, but Marcy gave him no chance.

"Do you know what it was like for them? Can you possibly understand how they felt when a policeman came to tell them that their mother and father were both dead? And poor little Ginger still doesn't understand what that means. She still thinks somebody's going to take her to her mother." The tears were almost spilling over now. Prescott took a handkerchief and offered it to her. She brushed his hand away, plucked a tissue from the box on her desk and blew her nose.

"Of course, I realize how they must have felt. That's why I came here as quickly as I could."

Marcy seemed not to hear him. "And how do you suppose they felt when a woman they didn't even know put them in a car and took them to another house to some other people they didn't know, either?" Her words came out fast and jumbled. "And now that they're beginning—just beginning, mind you—to adjust to these people, here you come! To carry them away to some other place! They've never seen you before in their lives. How do you think they'll feel when you...oh, if you really cared, you'd know...you'd know...." Her voice trailed off.

CHAPTER FOUR

HE COULDN'T BELIEVE THIS. She was actually crying—or about to cry, anyway. As though he were some kind of devil all set to pounce upon the children and drag them off to the gates of hell! Instead of an uncle who really cared, who was just as concerned as she was about the very things she mentioned. Didn't she realize that? Didn't she realize he'd come here because he thought those children needed him?

"Now just you listen to me," he started to say. Then stopped.

It wouldn't be so bad if she cried. Really cried. He could stand that. But she was fighting so valiantly for control. Trying to hold back the tears that shimmered in her eyes, turning them into iridescent pools of green.

"I'm sorry. I shouldn't have spoken to you like that."

She swallowed, and he saw her neck muscles tense, watched the rapid throb of the pulse in her throat. "I—I just want to make it easier for Ginger and Davey. I wish…" She turned away from him, hiding a grief that was as stark and real as his own.

He had a crazy impulse to hold her in his arms and comfort her, to cradle that tousled head against his chest and tell her everything was going to be all right. Damn it, everything *was* going to be all right!

"Mr. Prescott, I do think it's best for you to go out and see the children first." The supervisor's voice startled him. He had forgotten she was there.

"Yes," he said. "I suppose so."

"They really should have an opportunity to get to know you. That would make things easier for everyone. Then we can work from there. We really appreciate your coming and we'll speed things up as much as we can." She spoke quickly, with hardly a pause; he knew she was trying to give Marcy Wilson time to compose herself.

"Now…" She slipped off her glasses and smiled brightly up at him. "I know how anxious you are to see the children. I think Miss Wilson was planning to take you out there this morning."

"Yes." But he had the oddest feeling that Marcy no longer wanted to take him out to meet the children, that she didn't want him anywhere near them.

"If we're going, we'd better get started," she said. Without looking at him, she picked up her purse and walked briskly toward the door. He followed her, pausing briefly to thank the supervisor, though he wasn't sure just what he was thanking her for.

Marcy was strangely silent as they drove away, speaking only when she had to give him directions. He'd suggested they travel in his car when he saw her stop by a battered blue Volkswagen. He couldn't have stood the torture of being squeezed up in it. His nerves were stretched tight enough as it was. He'd been getting the third degree since he arrived, and after that scene this morning—damn it, what was he supposed to do to prove he was okay?

He glanced at her. The tears were gone, but she looked so subdued. Not at all like the sophisticated woman who had come into the office an hour ago, talking and smiling…. He found himself wishing he could bring the gaiety back.

"Miss Wilson, you needn't worry about the children," he said, keeping his eyes on the road. "I'll be good to them. I loved Diane, too, you know. I—"

"Yes, I know." She sounded detached.

"I know I'm not the world's best candidate for a father."

She said nothing and her silence irritated him.

"I'm sorry that I tried to rush you, but I do have to be in New York tomorrow. I can't put this meeting off any longer."

"I understand."

The hell you do! You've made up your mind against me. You think I'm a hard-nosed businessman who's trying to squeeze the children in between appointments. I put this meeting off twice. Dropped everything when I heard about Diane. There's six million riding on this merger and they're waiting for my decision. I can't leave them hanging any longer.

"Well," he said aloud, "since there seems no way around all this red tape, I can see I'm not going to get the kids tonight." He was aware that he was conceding, and it made him feel angry with himself. Still, he didn't have much choice. "I guess I'll just have to go to New York and come back here when I'm through."

"It's a shame you have to be so inconvenienced."

Was she being sarcastic? He shot her a quick glance, but he couldn't tell. She was looking out the window.

"I have to go," he said. "It's my job."

"Take the next exit."

He switched to the right lane and drove down the ramp.

"Now follow this avenue to the next corner," she directed. "Then turn right."

He found himself driving through a small community of modest tract houses. Some were freshly painted with neat, well-kept lawns. Others looked neglected—peeling paint, sagging screen doors and lawns that were more weeds than grass.

"Why did you pick this neighborhood?" he asked, when he noticed a couple of broken-down cars in one front yard.

"I choose people, not neighborhoods," she said quietly. "Turn here. It's toward the end of this block."

Suddenly he felt nervous. Diane's children. *They don't know me. They've never seen me before in their lives.* He wished now that they did know him. He wished he'd come to visit them when Diane was alive and happy. He wished he could believe they'd be glad to see him.

"Park here. That's the place."

It was one of the neater houses. But the signs of poverty were there. Well, what did he expect? People who kept other people's children too often did it because they needed the money. Nobody knew that better than he. Feverishly, he reached up to loosen his tie as the painful memory surfaced, almost choking him.

The year his father couldn't find anyone to live in and had boarded him and Diane with the Cooksons... He was eight years old at the time, and even now he could hear Mrs. Cookson's shrill voice, could feel her scrawny fingers biting into his shoulder while she looked sternly down at him.

"You keep your mouth shut, do you hear? Don't you tell Mr. Cookson that your pa was here today!"

Because that was the day Dad had brought the money. The Cooksons were always fighting about money and it scared him. He would grab Diane and run to the back of the yard until all the shouting was over. They were never really mean to him or Diane, but once his dad had left money for new tennis shoes and—

"Good afternoon, Miss Wilson. Why, I'd almost given up on you." A harried-looking woman holding a baby was opening the screen door. It led into a small, neatly furnished living room. Clean and cared for. Steve looked around but saw no sign of the children.

"Hello, Tina. How's my girl?" Marcy touched the baby on the chin and kissed a dimpled hand. "How's the teething?"

"Fine, since we got the teething gel." The woman glanced over at him as she spoke.

"Mrs. Jones," Marcy said, "this is Mr. Prescott, the Nelson children's uncle."

Mrs. Jones stretched out a work-worn hand to Steve. "Oh, those poor little tykes. They really need you. I'm so glad you've come."

"Thank you," he said, smiling. "It's nice that someone's glad," he added, avoiding Marcy's eyes.

Mrs. Jones looked a little puzzled. "Well, you folks just sit down," she said. "I'll go fetch the children. I had them all cleaned up before lunch, but...well, you know kids." She disappeared toward the back of the house and Steve turned to meet Marcy's scorching gaze.

"Don't be ridiculous," she snapped. "Of course I'm glad you came. I wouldn't want Diane's children shuffled around in the system for anything in the world. It's just that I want you to be more...more..."

"Sensitive?" he suggested.

"Oh, I suppose...well, yes."

"You don't give me much credit, do you? You think—"

"Marcy!" A tiny girl ran into the room and hurled herself into Marcy's arms, so quickly that he got only a glimpse of her—tangled yellow curls, soiled red coveralls.

He stared at the small figure huddled against Marcy and felt a rush of apprehension. She was so little.

The boy came more slowly, dragging his feet. Cautiously he seated himself on the edge of a chair against the opposite wall. He was holding something—a board?—grasping it firmly, as if for support. He said nothing but looked warily from Marcy to Steve and back again.

Steve's eyes misted and his chest throbbed. This was Diane's boy. Oh, yes! The dark hair and eyes, the set of his mouth. That penetrating look. Yes, even his jeans were slipping down and one scuffed sneaker was untied. Like Diane.

"Marcy," came the little girl's plaintive treble. "Davey and Troy won't let me play."

"She can't climb up to our tree house." Davey looked defensively at Marcy. "She's too little."

"I am *not* too little." She turned to face her brother, one hand brushing back the tumbled hair, and Steve could see that her face was smudged. And very pretty. But not at all like Diane's.

"I told you, Ginger. We're putting up steps. See?" Davey raised his board. "When we get done, then you can climb up. Okay?"

"'Kay." She dismissed him and turned back to Marcy. "Did you bring Lilli Ann?"

"And my dump truck?" asked Davey. "Me and Troy are digging a tunnel and we could—"

"Wait. Wait just a minute," Marcy said. "I told you that I can't get into your house yet. But your uncle can. Davey, Ginger, this is your uncle Stephen. Remember? I told you he was coming to see you."

Both children stared at him. Ginger's look was searching, Davey's still wary. *I must be careful,* Steve thought. He didn't want to overwhelm or frighten them. So he stayed, unmoving, in his chair.

"Hello," he said. And smiled.

Marcy had forgotten that smile, warm, unreserved, yet somehow vulnerable. She sensed his anxiety and found herself hoping that the children, too, would be touched.

"What's an uncle?" Ginger asked.

"That means he's your mommy's brother," Marcy explained, "like Davey is your brother."

"And I love you and want to take care of you." Steve slid from the chair and bent down, resting on his heels in front of Ginger. "Would you like to come and live with me?"

"Will you take me where my mommy is?"

Steve shot Marcy a look of such sheer panic that she answered for him. "No, sweetheart, he can't do that," she said, running her hand through Ginger's hair and trying to keep her own voice steady. "But he loves you very much—just like your mommy and daddy."

For an instant his expression revealed relief and gratitude, then he returned his attention to Ginger.

"I...we could go places and—" He gestured toward Davey, including him in the plans. "We could do things, the three of us. We'll have lots of fun, and..."

"Could I have a pony?" The question startled him, but before he could answer, Ginger prattled on. "Marcy took us to the park. And I rode on one, all by myself. I wasn't ascared. I didn't cry, did I, Marcy?"

"No, you didn't," Marcy answered.

"See?" Ginger appealed to Steve. "I'm not ascared. I like ponies."

Steve laughed. "Well, then, I guess a pony is something we definitely have to think about."

This obviously interested Davey. He climbed off his chair, walked over to Steve and looked directly at him. "Do you have any horses in your yard?"

"Well, no, but—"

"Then I think I'll stay here. We better stay here, Ginger."

Marcy was watching Steve's face. He looked absolutely crushed.

"But I'm your uncle. And I want you to—" He broke off when Marcy touched his arm.

"You kids think about it, and we'll talk later," she said quickly. "Your uncle and I will be back to see you soon. Say goodbye to him now."

"Can't we go home with you, Marcy?" Ginger asked.

"I'm sorry, sweetheart. Not now. Perhaps this weekend. Come and give me a goodbye kiss."

The little girl flung her arms around Marcy and kissed her warmly. Then she turned to bestow the same favor on Steve. Her action took him so completely by surprise that he toppled over, causing Ginger to giggle in delight.

"You should always give fair warning," he said, getting to his feet and smiling down at her.

Davey's goodbye was less exuberant. Still awkwardly holding his board, he offered his cheek for Marcy's kiss, then gravely shook Steve's hand.

Marcy said she had to speak with Troy for a minute, and followed the children out of the room.

Steve stared after them. Until now he had thought of them as, well, as "the kids"... Diane's kids, who'd suddenly become his responsibility. But he had been presented with two distinct and very different individuals. An effervescent, outgoing, talkative golden-haired girl who, tiny as she was, knew what she wanted and said so without hesitation. A lump rose in his throat. How could he make her understand about her mother? And Davey—a quiet thoughtful little boy who was as solemn as a man. But still a child, playing in tree houses, digging a tunnel. *We better stay here, Ginger.* He felt a surge of panic. Suppose they refused to come with him?

Marcy's voice broke into his thoughts. "All right. I'm ready." She slipped her bag over her shoulder and started for the door.

"Thank you for coming, Mr. Prescott." Mrs. Jones, still holding the baby, nodded to him. "I'll expect you back soon."

"Yes, thank you," said Steve. And then they were outside, walking toward the car.

"Marcy," Ginger called from the doorway, "don't forget to bring Lilli Ann."

"I won't forget," Marcy promised.

"Who's Lilli Ann?" asked Steve, as they got into the car.

"It's the Cabbage Patch doll she was given last Christmas. We haven't been able to enter the apartment to get any of their toys. But if you... You are going to the condo this afternoon?"

"Yes, I'm to see Sheriff Olsey at two to pick up the key."

Marcy thought of the abandoned Nelson apartment. That was going to be hard for him. She thought momentarily of accompanying him to make it easier.

Marcy, you get too involved. It was no business of hers.

"Well, I wish you'd look. You might find the doll in Ginger's room, under the bed, or almost anywhere. It's a big cloth doll with a plaid dress and floppy arms and legs, and a head full of yellow yarn."

"All right. A doll. I'll look for it." His mind seemed somewhere else. She saw his brow crease and his hands tighten on the steering wheel. "Look, Miss Wilson. The children. Do they have anything to do with this decision-making?"

"What do you mean?"

"I mean... Suppose they don't... Well, that is, could they refuse to come and live with me?"

"Oh. I see. Well, actually they have little to do with the decision." Her tone became mockingly professional. "It is our considered opinion that children under five are not capable of making such a long-term decision."

"Well, thank God for that!"

She laughed. "You mean you're afraid you can't compete? Don't you have a tree in that suite of yours?"

His smile was rueful. "No, and no pony, either. Maybe I could manage a pony in Central Park. And that might lure Ginger. But I get the feeling she always listens to her brother, and he—"

"Hey, listen. You have to give them a chance to know you. You only spent about five minutes with them. I had planned that we'd take them out for lunch today, but there wasn't time." She hesitated, then grinned. "Since you spent the whole morning being obnoxious."

He turned anxiously toward her, but chuckled when he saw her face. "Well, yes, I did get a little out of hand, didn't I?"

"You did."

"And I'm afraid I made both of us miss lunch. I'm sorry."

"Well, you can remedy that. There's a deli right next to the office. Quick service. You could still make it to your appointment."

As they took their place in line at the deli, Marcy wondered why she felt so relaxed and friendly toward him now. This morning she could have slugged him and never looked back. But now he seemed...likable. Perhaps it had something to do with the way he'd responded to the children. He'd been so reticent and anxious and...well, he acted as though he really cared. And now he was afraid they wouldn't like him.

"I'm sorry I was so obnoxious this morning," he said as they seated themselves with their sandwiches and drinks. "It's just that I rushed here expecting to find two desperate kids. I thought they'd be frightened and crying. I didn't expect to find them so contented."

"Children have a way of coping," she said. "Sometimes even better than grown-ups."

"It looks that way. They seemed...almost happy."

Marcy swallowed a bit of pastrami sandwich before she spoke. "You can thank Sarah Jones for that. She has a knack for making children immediately feel comfortable. That's why she's in emergency care."

"Emergency?"

"An emergency placement is when a child has to be removed from his home quickly and suddenly, usually in a traumatic situation. Like Ginger and Davey." She took a sip of her Coke. "Mrs. Jones has another boy whom you didn't see. His mother was hospitalized and there was no one to care for him. But thank goodness, she's recovering nicely, so he can go home soon."

Steve seemed to be studying Marcy, gazing intently at her as she spoke. "You really care, don't you?" It was more a statement than a question, and she felt a little embarrassed.

"It's my job, sir," she quipped. *Someone has to care.*

"And the baby?" he asked.

"Tina? Well…" Slowly Marcy stirred the ice in her drink with a straw. She felt a little sick as she remembered the day Tina had been brought in to the agency. The big eyes and thin little face, the bloated belly, the scars of abuse. Fortunately, a neighbor had called Protective Services. "Tina had been neglected," she told him, "but now her mother has released her for adoption." Marcy brightened at the thought. Sometimes it took a crisis to bring about a better situation for the child. "Adoption already has a family that wants her. Just as soon as we can find the father and get his release. So in a little while she'll be out of the system."

"The system? You mentioned that before."

"The foster parent system."

"I see. Well, if you screen your foster parents as carefully as you do a prospective guardian uncle, every placement must be perfect."

She looked up to see if he was joking, but his face was unreadable. "We try. We really do try," she repeated with emphasis. "But it's not always perfect." So many children. So few good homes. If she had her way, she'd make some really big changes. But there was no need to foist the problems of a frustrated social worker on this man. "It's almost two. You'd better go and meet the sheriff." She put down her napkin and stood up to leave. "Thanks for lunch."

"Wait." He caught her hand and she felt an odd quickening in her pulse. "Do you think I'll have a problem?" He looked earnestly up at her. "I mean if my references are okay, am I going to have any trouble getting my kids?"

His kids. He was already thinking of them as his. She liked that. And she might as well be honest. Ginger and Davey did not belong in the system—not when there was a relative who was willing and financially able to assume responsibility.

"Well, no, I don't expect that you'll have any real problem." She looked down at the hand that enveloped hers, giving her a strange feeling of intimacy. "But—now, don't misunderstand me—but I think it would really help your situation if you came up with some plans. That way, when you go before the judge, you'll have some answers. You'll know where you're going to take the children and how you'll arrange for their daily care."

"Thanks. I'll do that." He hesitated. "I really do appreciate the advice. And I'm sorry I was so difficult this morning." He smiled, gripping her hand tighter. "Friends?"

"Friends," she said.

IT WAS MORE than just a matter of picking up the key from Sheriff Olsey. It involved a call to his New York lawyer, who then called a local lawyer, followed by a trip to the courthouse where he was officially made "temporary administrator (pending investigation)." Only then was he given the key to his sister's apartment.

Sheriff Olsey furnished him with clear directions to the Woodside complex, so Steve found it without difficulty. He was immediately struck by the country atmosphere and the beauty of the natural surroundings. *It's well-planned—doesn't look crowded,* he thought, as he drove through the winding grounds looking for the designated parking area. When he got out of the car, a man who was getting into a blue station wagon gave him a friendly nod. Steve returned the salute, locked his car and started up the path. The sounds of the station wagon had faded, and except for the chirping of the birds and the crunch of his footsteps on the gravel path, all was quiet. Funny, that silence in the middle of an apartment complex. But he liked the feeling. He remembered something in one of Diane's letters. "It's so quiet and serene here," she'd written. "Good for the children..." *Diane.*

He walked up the five steps and along the wooden ledge to number 212. He took a deep breath, braced himself, then unlocked the door and opened it cautiously.

Once inside, he leaned against the door, his heart pounding, and looked slowly around. He was in a living room, quite spacious and very bright. A large comfortable sofa lined one wall. It was occupied by a fuzzy brown bear whose glass eyes stared at him. There was a magazine lying open on the coffee table and a white bowl containing dead roses. He breathed in the sweet musty smell of the decaying roses, and imagined Diane arranging them, humming a little tune as she did so, never knowing....

It was so still. He moved, wanting to break the silence, but his feet made no sound on the thick carpet. His foot struck something—a tiny train lying on its side. He picked it up, laid it carefully on the coffee table.

The room was bright, he realized, because the back wall was solid glass and there were no draperies. Sliding doors opened onto a patio where he could see a glass-topped wrought-iron table and four chairs. Almost in a trance, he walked through the apartment. It was exceptionally large, with four bedrooms.

One of the smaller bedrooms had evidently been David's office. There was a well-filled bookcase, the top shelf of which held several books—*Dead Summer*, *Killjoy*, *Death On A Ramp* and others—all by David Nelson. The guy was prolific, Steve thought. And successful. Diane and the children had not been in need. In fact, from the look of the place, they'd been well-cared-for. Steve was glad about that.

On the desk was a typewriter with a half-typed page in it, an empty coffee cup and a picture of Diane. She was leaning against a boat, laughing. Steve picked up the picture and stared at it for a long time, before carefully and tenderly replacing it. Then he walked slowly out of the room, taking care to step over a half-finished jigsaw puzzle of Donald

Duck. A child had lain on the floor, fitting in the pieces while her father typed.

I like you, David Nelson. I never knew you, but I like you. Because you made Diane happy. Because this is a happy home.

He remembered that he was to look for a doll called Lilli Ann and went back into what was obviously Ginger's room to find it. He looked everywhere—in the toy box, on the shelves, even under the bed. There were several dolls, but none like the one Miss Wilson—Marcy—had described. He wondered if he should take any of the others. Well, when he came back from New York, he'd make a more thorough search.

He wandered back into the master bedroom, wanting to capture the essence of Diane that seemed to linger there. He inhaled the sweet feminine scent of powder and perfume, saw the pale pink robe thrown across the rumpled bed, the red and white sandal lying askew on the floor. He found himself staring at the sandal. It awakened a memory, vague and sweet, a long-ago memory buried deep inside him. His mother, laughing gaily as she tossed one shoe after another across the room. Trying to find just the right pair, because one of the uncles was coming. There had been several uncles.

"Stevie, honey, you be a good boy, and help Mary take care of your little sister. I'll be back soon. Now, give me a big hug and a kiss."

He would hug her, savoring the special fragrance that was hers. Then he'd count the minutes until her return. She would come in, smiling and happy, ready to play some game or sing a silly song. She never once told him not to tell his dad about the uncles. But he never did. Not even that last time when she went off with one of the uncles and didn't come back.

He didn't say anything when his dad told them that their mother was dead. But he knew she wasn't dead. For a long time he kept waiting for her to come back. But she never did.

And now this room of Diane's reminded him. His mother would have worn such a robe. He reached across to pick up the flimsy material, and as he did, he uncovered something else—a floppy cotton leg, a scrap of red plaid. He straightened up and removed the pillow. He'd found Lilli Ann.

He could almost visualize that last morning. Ginger had probably come into her parents' room, dragging her doll. She'd climbed into bed with her mother just as, long ago, he'd sometimes climbed into bed with his mother. Diane had pulled her daughter close. And Ginger had been happy, basking in the warmth and the love, and the sweet delicate scent. And she had thought that it would last forever. That people who loved you would not go away.

Ginger's mother did not have a choice. He knew that his own mother did, and the knowledge was a pain that had haunted him all of his life.

Suddenly he could hold back the tears no longer, and he broke down. The great racking sobs almost tore him apart, but he wasn't sure whether he cried for the loss of Ginger's mother or his own.

CHAPTER FIVE

MARCY STOPPED by the grocery store on her way home from work. A careful survey of her bank account had warned her that if she wanted to eat regularly between now and her next paycheck, she'd better start fixing her own meals. She could live for a week on the cost of two dinners at Sutton's. She wheeled her cart toward the vegetable bins, trying to figure out where the money had gone. She'd thought she was in pretty good shape.

Well, there were the shoes she didn't need but hadn't been able to resist. And the two or three long-distance telephone calls to Jennifer. What else? The tickets for the circus. But that wasn't too much. And...oh, yes, the calculator for Jimmy Braxton. Odd birthday present to be giving a ten-year-old, she supposed. But that was what he wanted, and she knew there was no money in the Emory budget for such a trinket. Mrs. Emory had mentioned that she planned to bake a birthday cake on Thursday and Marcy hoped to get the pocket calculator to him by then.

"Marcy Wilson, if you're going to survive in this business, you'd better learn to leave your work at the office!" Marcy could almost hear Jo Stanford's voice. "Get your mind off these children and their problems. Think about something pleasant for a change."

Something pleasant... Like Steve Prescott, for example. She liked him. She really did. Marcy smiled as she selected three firm tomatoes and placed them in her cart. If anybody had asked her at ten o'clock that morning for her opinion of Stephen Prescott, her response would hardly have been complimentary. But when she'd seen him with the children, so awkward and uncertain, so anxious to please, her heart had gone out to him.

Anxiety. That's what had made him so irritable this morning. He'd turned out to be quite different from what she'd expected. What was it she'd told herself? Steve Prescott "wouldn't feel obliged to do anything!" But obviously, he did. And it was more than a sense of duty. He seemed to really care. He wanted the children, never mind that he didn't have the slightest idea what he was going to do with them when he got them!

She would have laughed had she not been so worried about it herself. Ginger and Davey had had such a good home, such loving parents. And now, even though they seemed to be coping, Davey had that wary look, and Ginger was still waiting for her mommy to come back. Marcy sighed. Now they were to be transferred to an entirely new environment with an uncle who had absolutely no experience in dealing with children.

None of that would be a problem if she could adopt the children herself. Or if Jennifer... Marcy's thoughts reverted to the last time she and Jennifer had discussed the question. She remembered how disturbed she'd been by her sister's apathy that day. *We need to talk,* she decided. *I'll drive out there this Sunday—and I'll take the kids with me.*

After that, she concentrated on her shopping. Salad fixings and lots of fruit. She bought a pound of ground beef that she planned to separate into patties and freeze. She hesitated over a package of four lamb chops. Expensive. But she could freeze those, too; that meant four meals. And since she wasn't going to be eating out ... She tossed the package into her cart and wheeled it toward the register, then headed home.

When she reached her apartment, she set the two bags on the floor and rummaged through her purse for the key. She was just inserting it in the lock when she saw Steve Prescott emerge from the apartment next door.

"Hello, again," she said.

He didn't seem to hear her.

"Hello," she repeated, more loudly this time.

"Oh. Hello." His voice sounded bleak, and he looked...lost. She had the feeling he was seeing not her but something else. She was startled by the naked pain in his face; she wanted to reach out, to ward off whatever was hurting him. He was walking past her now, and she tugged impulsively at his sleeve.

"Wait," she said. "Give me a hand, will you?"

"What?"

"With these groceries." She picked up one of the bags and handed it to him so purposefully that he was forced to take it. "I had a heck of a time lugging these from the car. Come on in."

For a moment she thought he wasn't going to move.

"Come in," she said again, and this time he followed her.

"Just put it here," she directed, setting her own bag on the dinette table. But he just stood there, holding the bag, looking dazed. She took it from him and put it next to hers. Something was dreadfully wrong.

"Sit down," she urged, pulling out a chair. "You look ... tired."

He said nothing, but he did sit down. She wondered what to do now. Offer him a drink, perhaps? Did she have any brandy in the house? She hurried into the little kitchenette and searched through the cabinets. A few weeks before, Tom had brought over a bottle of brandy. Oh yes, here it was. She filled a small brandy glass almost to the brim, then brought it over to him.

"Oh, thanks," he said, looking surprised.

"Just relax while I put these groceries away." She carried the bags into the kitchen and started to unload them, glancing at him from time to time through the opening above the breakfast bar. He sat quite still, staring out the window, only occasionally remembering to take a sip of the brandy.

Something had hit him hard! She'd known that going through the apartment would be difficult for him. But there was more to this, more even than grief. Guilt? Possibly, Marcy thought. Guilt for not having come more often when Diane was alive.

Marcy took out the pound of hamburger and put it in the refrigerator. She'd separate it later. She took out the package of lamb chops, then she looked across at him. If he intended to drive to Sacramento tonight, he'd need some time to settle down and compose himself.

"I think I'll treat you to dinner," she called. He didn't answer and she wasn't sure he'd even heard her.

Well, Marcy decided, she certainly wasn't going to cook dinner in her Liz Claiborne coatdress. He didn't even look up when she passed him on her way to the stairs. In her loft bedroom, she changed into jeans and a rose-colored pullover.

Back in the kitchen, she prepared two potatoes, put them in the microwave and set the timer. She sprinkled all four lamb chops with seasoned salt and slid them under the broiler, then began to wash the lettuce.

THE MICROWAVE BUZZER went off, startling Stephen, and he sat up. Where was he? He looked around and his gaze fastened on Marcy, busy in the kitchen. Gradually it came back to him. He'd helped her in with her groceries. But how long had he been sitting here? He stared down at the empty glass. Brandy. Yes, she'd given it to him, he remembered that now. His mind had been years away. Because of Diane's room...

Well, he couldn't sit here thinking about it. He'd better leave—right now. He picked up the glass, hesitated a moment, then walked quickly to the kitchen. She was putting ice into two tall glasses, and he noticed that she'd changed her clothes. She looked like a teenager in those jeans and that pink pullover.

"Thanks," he said, giving her the empty glass. "I really needed that. I'll check with you when I get back. I remember what you suggested, and I'll get back here as soon as I can."

"You're not going?" she asked. "I've almost got your dinner ready."

"Dinner? You're fixing dinner for me?"

She nodded as she poured iced tea into the glasses.

"I invited and you accepted. So you can't leave yet."

He frowned. "I don't remember anything about dinner." He hadn't been that out of it, had he?

"You accepted and I cooked. So, be a good sport and make yourself useful." She was handing him place mats and napkins, but he backed away. For some reason, he was irritated by her coaxing tone.

"Look, I don't have time for dinner," he insisted. "I have a plane to catch."

She stood there, holding the napkins, looking puzzled.

"But it doesn't leave until tomorrow morning. You have plenty of time."

He realized that he'd shouted at her, and felt a little ashamed.

"I don't understand. What's the problem?" she asked. "You said you were hungry. It's just dinner."

"Right." He took the things from her. Why *was* he making such a big fuss? Mats here. And here. Napkins. It was just that he found this whole setup a little too cozy and intimate. No, intimate wasn't the word. He'd been intimate with women before. But never close. And he meant to keep it that way. That was it. There was something about this woman, a concern, a caring quality that touched him, and—

"Silver's in the side drawer!" she called.

Officious, he thought, jerking the drawer open. *She's too damned officious!* Had he said he was hungry?

Well, he hadn't actually said he was hungry and he didn't agree to stay for dinner, Marcy thought, as she took the chops out of the oven. *But he does need time, and this will give him a couple of hours to come to grips with whatever is troubling him.*

Not bad, Marcy, not bad, she told herself when she'd put the food on the plates. The lamb chops looked and smelled delicious, the butter was melting in the steaming potatoes, and the salad was crisp and colorful.

"Dinner's ready," she announced as she carried the plates into the dining nook and set them on the table. "Why not take off your coat and tie? Make yourself comfortable."

He did as she suggested, but she wondered at the guarded look he gave her and was tempted to call out, "Hey, I'm on your side." But she didn't.

Instead, during dinner, she launched into small talk—the weather, the book she'd just read, the play she'd seen the week before. Anything to distract him from whatever had troubled him so deeply. He answered in monosyllables and she was aware that he was only half listening. It wasn't until she paused, searching her mind for another safe topic, that he finally spoke.

"This is a very good dinner," he said, as if he'd suddenly remembered his manners, "and very kind of you, Miss Wilson."

"It's Marcy, please. Outside the office I'm Marcy."

"Yes, I suppose it should be Marcy and Steve by this time. Do you realize every meal I've had in this town has been with you? I can't help feeling that's an imposition."

"Nonsense," she said, glad to see even a trace of that smile reappear. "Turnabout is fair play. You paid for the other two, remember?" Then she frowned. "Do you mean to say you didn't eat breakfast this morning? No wonder you were so grouchy."

"Well..." This time the smile was rueful. "I was in a hurry. I wanted to—"

"Get the children and get out of here," she teased.

"Well, yes. I didn't realize it was going to be so complicated." Now he looked worried, and she was instantly contrite, sorry she'd brought up the very subject that was obviously weighing on his mind.

"Not so complicated," she said. "All you have to do is—"

"Figure out where I'm going to take them and who'll look after them," he broke in rather sharply. "That's not easy. I think my hotel suite would give them claustrophobia. And it's going to take time to find the right person and the right schools. I have a friend who lives in Scarsdale, and I thought I could ask her about all this. But I hate to impose on her."

Of course, he would have a "friend." Marcy wondered why the thought depressed her.

"She'd probably be glad to help you. That's what friends are for, isn't it?"

"Well, I don't know if she... Actually, it's Brick who's my friend. My partner. He's president of Semco. When he called me about tomorrow's meeting, he told me that he and Stell, his wife, had split up and he'd moved out. Moved *in* actually." Steve grinned. "He told me he was at my place."

"I see." Marcy felt ridiculously lighthearted. Strangely glad that Brick was the friend, and that he'd felt free to move into Steve's suite...which meant there was no one else living there, didn't it? She felt herself flush. *Detachment, Marcy, detachment. So what if he has a special smile? In a few weeks he'll be nothing but a fond memory.*

"You shouldn't worry," she said, getting up to clear the table. "Things will work out. You've only had...let's see...not even a week. Hardly long enough to think, much less plan. Give yourself time. No, don't bother with the dishes. I'll do that. You go on into the living room. We'll have our coffee there. Coffee and some old-fashioned tea cakes. I bought them at the bakery next to the deli." She realized she was talking too much. It was a relief to escape to the kitchen where she could concentrate on making coffee. Instead of thinking about Steve Prescott.

" 'Give yourself time,' she says. But time is just what I don't have," Steve muttered, as he stood in Marcy's living room. Her apartment was smaller than the one next door and was done in muted tones of mauve and slate blue. He watched her come in to set a percolator on the hearth and plug it into the wall socket. There was a certain confidence about her, a quiet poise in everything she did. She seemed, somehow, to be at total peace with herself. She looked as right in those jeans as she had in the sophisticated garb of the morning. He got the impression that she would be no less relaxed before a camp fire in Peru than she was at this moment in her comfortable living room.

"While that perks, I'll get the tea cakes." She straightened up and went back into the kitchen.

When she returned, he was studying one of the pictures on the wall by the fireplace. He thought it looked like a crude charcoal sketch of . . . well, he couldn't quite decide. What was it supposed to be? A man riding a bicycle upside down? A horse lying on its back? A knight in armor falling off his horse—upside down? He bent his head to examine it the other way around, but he still couldn't make sense of it.

"Another original from some kid whose path has crossed yours?" he asked.

She smiled as she set her tray on the coffee table. "Why, my good sir," she said, "I'll have you know that drawing is an original Picasso!"

"Picasso?" He stared at her in amused amazement. Then he turned back to view the picture, tightening his lips and assuming a pose of mock appreciation. "I see. It's looking better all the time."

Her peal of laughter delighted him.

"It only proves," she said, "that you can get away with anything if you're famous enough."

Over the coffee and cakes, she explained that all the pictures were from her parents' home. When her father died, her mother had sold the house and divided all the treasures among her three children—Bill, an air force officer currently stationed with his family in Japan, Jennifer, who lived with her husband in Shingle Springs, and Marcy. She'd then moved into a retirement community in Phoenix. Yes, Marcy said, the family was from Phoenix; she'd lived there all her life until she'd finished college and gone away to work.

"Goodness," she said finally, "I don't know why I'm doing all this talking about myself."

But Steve knew why. He had prompted her, and deliberately drawn her out, just as he was accustomed to drawing out a prospective investor, looking into his background before accepting his check. There was no reason to be curious about Marcy. But her serene self-confidence intrigued him. And now he knew how it had been acquired. A happy, stable middle-class home, a direct contrast to his own confused and impoverished childhood. Hers had obviously been secure, sheltered…loving. And that's what he wanted for Ginger and Davey.

I promise you they will have it, Diane. But how? Where do I start?

Abruptly he rose to his feet. "I've got to get the children. I want to get Ginger and Davey as quickly as possible."

Marcy sat up, startled by the urgency in his voice.

"What's the matter? I thought we'd agreed—"

"Oh, I don't mean today. I've given up on that. I'm going along with all this legal rigmarole, but I want to get them as soon as possible." He shoved his hands in his pockets, jingling his change in nervous frustration as he looked down at her. "Don't you understand? They don't know me. And the longer they stay at this Jones woman's house, the harder it's going to be for them to get close to me. Don't you see?"

She nodded, setting her mug on the tray. Her calmness suddenly irritated him and he moved restlessly about.

"Of course I understand how you feel," she was saying. "But can't you see that careful preparation facilitates a smoother transition?"

Facilitates a smoother transition! Damn all that bureaucratic jargon when he was thinking about the children!

"But I don't have time!" he almost shouted as he ran a distracted hand through his hair. "Sure, I can buy a house in Scarsdale or somewhere. And sure, I can interview housekeepers. But all of this takes a lot of time. Don't you see?" He walked to the fireplace and back, then said in a resigned voice, "Guess I'll just have to move them into my suite temporarily."

"Two bedrooms, did you say?" She wasn't looking at him, but seemed to be intently studying her nails. "I presume your friend will be leaving. Even so, you'd hardly have room for a live-in, a necessity in your case."

He glared at her, annoyed by her logic and, even more, by the fact that she was right.

"What about a larger apartment?" she suggested. "Some temporary place until you buy?"

"Well, yes, I suppose." He clenched and unclenched his fists, feeling at a loss. Where did people with children live in New York? Brick was the only person he knew who had a child and—

"Steve!" she cried. She jumped to her feet, staring at him, her eyes wide. "How often did you say you were in New York?"

"Oh, I don't know. Maybe a month or two out of the year. Off and on."

"Then you could make your home almost anywhere, couldn't you?" She sounded eager. "I mean on a temporary basis."

"Well, yes, I suppose I could, but—"

"So why don't you live here?"

"Here?"

"I mean next door, in David and Diane's place. It would be..." She touched a finger to her temple. "Oh, why didn't I think of this before? It would be so good for the children. They'd be coming home. They'd be in familiar surroundings and have all their own toys, be in their own rooms. It would make things so much easier for them."

He stood with his thumbs hooked into his belt, gazing down at the floor. Moving into Diane's place was certainly a possibility, but ... why did he feel he was being manipulated?

"Don't you see?" she burst out. "They could go back to the same schools—Davey's kindergarten, Ginger's nursery school. The same teachers and friends."

And you, he thought. You'd be right next door, holding on to them. And checking up on me.

"You don't trust me to take them away from your watchful eye?" he asked.

"Don't be ridiculous! It's not a watchful eye but a helping hand that you need. And," she added, with a little gurgle of laughter, "helping is my business."

"Your business is to shuffle papers and stretch red tape!" he snapped. "Diane's children are my business."

She put her hands on her hips and glared up at him. "Stephen Prescott, that's unfair. I care about those children."

"And it would be very convenient, wouldn't it, to have them right next door to you!"

"And very convenient for you as well."

He stepped back. "And just what is that supposed to mean?"

"It means—" she began, counting on her fingers "—one, that you have satisfactorily solved the problem of a proper domicile. Two, that the children will not be uprooted. And three, that your pressing need for time has been solved. Here's a place, ready and waiting, that will give you time to establish a relationship with the children, while you search for a permanent residence.''

For a moment he stood perfectly still, thinking. It did make sense. But who the hell did she think she was—dishing out all the answers as if he couldn't manage his own affairs! He walked briskly over to the couch and picked up his jacket.

"I'll have to think about that," he said. "Anyway, I plan to look around for a place while I'm in New York."

"Do that. You might find something much more suitable." As sweet as she sounded, he thought he detected a note of sarcasm in her voice. He turned quickly, but she was smiling.

"I'm planning to see the children this weekend," she said. "Did you find Lilli Ann?"

Lilli Ann. He stiffened, feeling it all come back to him. The robe. The sandal on the floor.

"Yes," he said, fingering the key in his jacket pocket. "I found her—on the bed in Diane's bedroom." He didn't want to go back in there.

"Do you mind?" he asked, handing her the key.

"Of course not," she said. "I'll pick up the doll and I'll look for Davey's dump truck too."

"Thanks." He started for the door, then turned around again. "Listen, would you . . ." He hesitated. Was this too much to ask? But he didn't want to go back into that room until there was no trace of Diane. Of anyone.

"Yes?" she prompted.

"Diane's clothes. And David's too. You're in welfare. Do you know someone who could use them? Or some place to take them?"

"Well, maybe. I could certainly ask."

"If you would and if you could get rid of them, I'd appreciate it. Get someone to help you. I'll pay for it. I just don't want . . . the truth is, I found those personal things upsetting. And I think it would be upsetting for the children if I do decide—and mind you, I haven't made a decision yet. But if I do decide to bring them here, I'd prefer there was nothing to remind us."

She was looking at him very hard. "Sure," she said. "I understand. I'll take care of it."

"Thank you. I'll be in touch."

CHAPTER SIX

IDIOT, MARCY THOUGHT, as she carefully refrained from slamming the door behind Steve. What was wrong with the man? He admitted that he didn't have a place for the kids to live. And he certainly didn't know the first thing about taking care of them. Yet, when presented with an intelligent and practical plan, he instantly rejected it! Possibly only because it was *her* suggestion.

But you'd better be careful, Stephen Prescott! She who shuffles the papers controls the world . . . well, at least that part of the world that concerns you. And you'd just better come up with a good plan for those two children!

It *was* true that she liked the idea of Ginger and Davey staying next door, where she could continue to see them and . . . *Detachment, Marcy.* But she did love the children, and Diane and David had been her friends, and she somehow felt she owed them something.

But it's their idiot uncle's decision, not yours. So forget it, Marcy Wilson.

However, she couldn't forget it, and she spent a very restless night. So, early the next morning, she phoned Gerald to arrange a prework game of tennis. Whacking a tennis ball around always cleared her head, and it was so easy to be able to call on Gerald.

"I don't know how you do it," Jo Stanford had once commented.

"Do what?" Marcy asked.

"Maintain good relationships with several men at the same time, while holding them all at arm's length."

"Oh, it's easy," Marcy had said breezily. "You just establish the ground rules right at the beginning."

But it wasn't always easy. Not when one of the parties became serious. Like Tom... Tom was showing signs of possessiveness. But with Gerald, there was never that worry. He had all he could do for the present, supporting himself and his ailing father, and he was as anxious as Marcy to maintain a "just friends" relationship.

The rest of the week passed in a flurry of interviews, meetings and reports. On Thursday, Marcy picked up Jimmy Braxton at school, took him out for hamburgers and gave him his birthday gift. Maybe, she thought, looking at his worn jeans and the way his arms extended beyond his jacket sleeves, she should have given him clothes instead. But...no. She was glad she'd chosen the calculator when she saw how elated he was. And she would speak to Mrs. Emory about his clothes. The Emorys had several foster children as well as their own large brood, and Marcy suspected that the entire check went toward basic household necessities, since she knew Mr. Emory had been out of work for some time now. She'd try to request a special clothing allowance for Jimmy, she decided.

Still, Marcy felt a little sad when she dropped Jimmy off at the house. She realized that the Emorys simply couldn't give him the loving attention he needed so badly. She would have preferred to move him, but it was difficult to find just the right place.

Anyway, she comforted herself as she drove away, Robert and Joyce Emory weren't undesirable foster parents. It was just that their own circumstances were difficult, and they simply didn't have the time or the training to respond to the emotional problems of such an active and demanding little boy.

Marcy knew that Jimmy yearned for the mother from whom he'd been taken two years before. Though shamefully lacking in the food and shelter department, Jimmy's mother, even through her drunken stupors, had managed to maintain a loving relationship with her son. But when Mrs. Braxton had disappeared for a week during one of her binges, leaving the boy to fend for himself, Protective Services had stepped in. Jimmy had been placed in the first of a series of foster homes; since then, he'd always been adequately cared for—but not with a parent's love. This was what Jimmy missed. And this was not easy to find.

On Saturday, Tom Jenkins took Marcy to dinner and to the symphony and told her more than she wanted to know about stocks and bonds.

On Sunday, Marcy drove to Shingle Springs to visit her sister, taking Ginger and Davey with her, as she'd planned. This turned out not to have been such a good idea. It rained steadily all day and the children couldn't play outside. Jennifer was worried about the damage they might do to her house. Ginger spilled punch on the linen tablecloth, and when Davey said the spaghetti was yukky, she wouldn't eat it either. Jenny had no peanut butter, so Marcy made toasted cheese sandwiches for the children.

After lunch, Jennifer spent half her time nagging the children to sit still and watch television, and the other half complaining to Marcy about Al, who'd left for the golf course early that morning. "How can he be playing golf when it's raining cats and dogs?" she whined.

If I were Al, Marcy thought ruefully, as she loaded the children into the Volkswagen, I think I'd spend my Sundays on the golf course, too. Rain or not. What on earth had given her the idea that Jennifer could adopt *any* child? Marcy's vague unease about her sister was rapidly becoming a full-blown anxiety. What was changing Jennifer from the warm, fun-loving girl who, three years before, had captured the heart of handsome Alfred R. Baker, one of the area's most successful real-estate developers? She'd had a spectacular wedding and then moved to that spacious home in Shingle Springs. Personally, Marcy had always considered Al a little too cocky, but Jennifer couldn't see the faults for the stars in her eyes. Had the romance faded? Perhaps Jennifer was growing bored with her comfortable life; perhaps she and Al had quarreled. Marcy worried about the sister who had always been so close. In fact, Marcy had transferred to the Auburn office mainly to be near Jennifer.

Her sister was just bored, Marcy decided, and that was what made her so irritable. She needed some activity of her own. Well, she and Al belonged to that exclusive racket club with the indoor courts. She would call Jennifer and arrange to play with her next Sunday. Then they could have lunch and a long, long talk—the talk they somehow hadn't got around to having that afternoon.

On Wednesday, she received a call from New York. She recognized the husky voice, and there was a little catch in her throat as she answered. "Yes, this is Marcy Wilson."

"Steve Prescott here. I've been thinking over what you said. Do you think it would speed things up if I changed my address to 212 Woodside?"

Was he bargaining with her?

"Possibly," she answered, unable to stem the tide of joy that was sweeping through her. She told herself it was because the children would still be living next door.

"Then please go ahead and change my address on the petition. I'll be there sometime this weekend. Do you think we might get things settled by the first of next week?"

"That depends on how soon your references get here. But otherwise there would be no problem. Though you'll still have to hire someone...." She paused, remembering that Mrs. Fisher, the office cleaning woman, had mentioned a sister who might be interested. "Would you like me to look around for a housekeeper?'' she asked, then wanted to bite her tongue when he answered.

"Thank you, no. My attorney has already contacted an agency in the area. They'll send someone out when I arrive."

Well, la-de-da. I hope your attorney knows what he's doing. She must remember to keep hands off.

"Very well then," she said. "That's taken care of. I'll concentrate on the paperwork." She emphasized the last word, but he didn't seem to notice.

"Er...there is one other thing. Did you find someone who could use the clothes?''

"Yes, as a matter of fact, I did. Someone who works here. Mrs. Fisher. She's coming out this afternoon."

"Good." She could hear the relief in his voice. "Thanks. I appreciate your taking care of it. I know it's a bit of trouble."

"I'm glad to do it," she said.

STEVE ARRIVED at the Sacramento airport late Saturday evening. It was raining, a drizzling, melancholy sort of rain, and there was a noticeable chill in the air. He picked up a rental car and drove to Auburn.

Actually it wasn't only Marcy's suggestion that had prompted him to take up residence at Woodside. While he was in New York, he'd had a chance to look at Diane and David's mail, which had been released to him from the Auburn post office. There was business he'd have to take care of. Bank statements indicated large sums of money in three accounts, as well as a safety deposit box. They had not had the good sense to make a will, but Dave did have mortgage insurance on the condo. Steve wanted to convert all the assets into trust funds for the children. Since there was no will, the state would have to get involved and...well, it was better for him to remain in California until things were settled. It wasn't because *she* had suggested he move into Woodside.

Still, as he neared Auburn, he found himself looking forward to seeing her. He wanted to ask her about the robot, which converted into a truck, that he'd bought for Davey. And the stuffed leopard for Ginger. The man at the store had said those were right for their age groups, but Marcy knew the kids. He was a little uncertain about the leopard. He thought Ginger might prefer a pony, but the stuffed ponies hadn't seemed very soft or cuddly. Anyway, it was a *real* pony that she'd set her heart on. And he wanted to ask Marcy if he should take the toys to the children immediately, or save them for a surprise when they came home.

When he reached Woodside, he left the toys in the car and bounded through the rain with his suitcase and garment bag. Since he had to get his key from Marcy first, he could ask her about the toys right away.

When he reached her apartment, he saw that the lights were on and he could hear laughter inside. He hesitated before he pressed the bell. A moment later, the door was opened by a man almost as tall as he, wearing a dark blue suit and thick horn-rimmed glasses.

"Yes?" said the man.

"I'm Steve Prescott. I wanted to see Miss Wilson."

"Who is it, Tom?" Marcy called.

The man stepped back and opened the door a little wider. Steve could see Marcy now. She was wearing something soft in a deep rose color and she was sitting on the floor before a blazing fire. There were things scattered about—a chessboard, wineglasses, a tray with food on it.

"Someone named Steve." There was a question in the man's voice as he turned back to Marcy.

"Oh, Steve! You're here already. Good." Marcy stood up and he could see the rose-colored thing was a sort of pants outfit, all in one piece. The pants were baggy and cinched at the ankle and she was barefoot.

"Come on in and close the door, for goodness' sake."

He came in, still holding his bags, and the man shut the door.

"This is Steve Prescott, Tom. He's moving in next door. Steve—Tom Jenkins. Sit down," she said to Steve. "Wouldn't you like a glass of wine? Or maybe something hot. It's pretty chilly outside."

But pretty damn cozy in here, Steve thought. And she had introduced him to some other man the first day he met her, hadn't she?

"Yes . . . no, I mean—no, I don't want anything, thank you. I just wanted to pick up the key."

The men stood looking at each other while she fetched the key from the buffet. Steve had the definite feeling that this horn-rimmed character was sizing him up.

"Here you are," she said, as she handed him the key. "I think everything's going to work out just fine. Some of your references have already arrived."

"That's good," he said.

"Sure you won't stay and have a drink or something to eat? There's plenty of cheese and salami."

"No. No, thank you. I'd better go on in. Good night." He nodded to both of them, turned abruptly and went out.

He felt very much alone when the door closed behind him. He wondered why that bothered him; he usually liked being alone. It was just that he'd wanted to ask her about the toys, he told himself. And yes, he hated to go back into that apartment. He hoped she'd managed to get rid of those reminders.

He opened the door and fumbled for the light switch, then stared in surprise. It looked different. Tidy. No bear standing on the sofa. No toys lying around. No dead flowers. The bowl on the coffee table contained a large bunch of colorful fall leaves. In the bedroom the bed was neatly made, the closets bare. No toiletries. Nothing. The essence of Diane was almost gone, but he felt almost as sad as he had the week before, when the room was full of her presence. He walked through the apartment and found a certain comfort in little mementos—family photographs, plants Diane had tended, signs of the happiness that had once existed there.

The next morning when he went into the bathroom to shower and shave, he looked again at the freshly laundered towels hanging on the rack, the bar of still-wrapped soap on the basin. Someone had done a very thorough job. *She* had seen to that. Today was Sunday. He'd take her out for brunch and thank her. Later, they could go to visit the children. He whistled as he quickly showered and dressed—tan slacks, beige-and-brown striped sport shirt, dark brown cashmere pullover. Then he hurried over to knock on her door.

She wasn't at home. He checked the lobby and the laundry room. Maybe she'd just gone out on an errand. He hung around for a while, but when she still wasn't back at ten, he drove into Auburn, ate breakfast at Sutton's and walked around the little town.

He returned to Woodside at two, but she hadn't come home yet. Not that he particularly wanted to see her, he told himself. It was just that Marcy Wilson happened to be the only person he knew in this town. And he'd hoped she could accompany him when he went to see the children.

Well, he decided, she must be spending the day with one of her men friends, either that Gerald guy or Horn Rims. A thought jolted him. Horn Rims had probably spent the night, and they'd gone out together this morning, and... Oh, hell! He didn't need her to take him to see his own niece and nephew.

When he arrived at the Jones house, he found the children reluctant to come too close. A little shy—he could understand that. He pulled the leopard from the box and held it out to Ginger. She moved forward tentatively and took it, then backed away.

"It's nice," she said, stroking the soft, cuddly form.

"Say 'thank you,'" Davey prompted.

"Thank you," repeated Ginger. Then, "Where's Marcy? Why didn't she come?"

"Ah...she's busy today." He held the other box out to Davey. "Here's something for you, Davey."

Davey cautiously took the box and thanked him politely. And unenthusiastically.

"Well, open it," Steve said. "Let's see how it works."

Davey warmed up a bit as they played with the toy but wanted to go show it to Troy almost immediately.

Neither child seemed interested in going out to dinner with him. Mrs. Jones said she couldn't allow it anyway, without an okay from the agency. As Steve returned to the apartment, he wondered why he'd felt it necessary to rush back from New York.

MONDAY MORNING when Marcy left for work, she noticed that a sealed envelope had been slipped under her door. As she was late, she didn't open it until she got to the office. In the envelope were two fifty-dollar bills and a note:

Miss Wilson,
Whoever cleaned the apartment did an outstanding job.
Please see that they are properly compensated. Thank
you for disposing of the personal items.

S.P.

When Marcy got home that afternoon, she went first to Steve's door. He wasn't there, so she wrote on the back of the envelope:

Mrs. Fisher and I cleaned. She was glad to do it for the clothes, and I was glad to do it for Diane.

M.W.

She put the two bills back in the envelope and slipped it under his door.

As Marcy had predicted, everything went smoothly. Steve's references were excellent, Marcy sent in a Recommend Approval form, and without further delay, the judge declared Stephen Prescott legal guardian of the Nelson children.

Throughout the proceedings, however, Steve's attitude had been strangely cool and formal. Marcy was puzzled by this. Of course, they hadn't hit it off too well in the beginning, but she had since been very helpful to him and he *was* getting the children. Not that she cared what Stephen Prescott said or did, she told herself. But still, it seemed odd. She usually got on well with men.

"Too well," her mother had often said. "You treat them just like you do your brother." And when Marcy asked what was wrong with that, her mother had replied that if Mr. Right ever did come along, he just might be put off by being treated like a big brother.

Well, she certainly didn't intend to worry about Steve's attitude. She would just take her cues from him and stay out of his affairs. Except where it concerned the children, of course. She did think he was making a mistake, hiring that woman from the Alston Child Care Agency, and she was going to tell him so. Right now, in fact. She threw on a sweater, marched resolutely to his apartment and firmly rang the bell.

"Don't stop what you're doing," she told him when he opened the door. "I know you're getting things ready for the children. But I wanted to talk about something."

"Okay," he said. "Come on in. I'm just packing up David's manuscripts to send to his agent."

"All of them?" she asked, watching him take papers from the filing cabinet and stack them into cartons.

"Yep. He says he has someone who can finish or revise all the unsold material, and he thinks it will sell. If so, that would add to the children's legacy." He paused, then looked at her anxiously, as if seeking confirmation. "I think this is what David would want, don't you?"

"Yes," she agreed. "I'm sure that's what he'd want."

"I'm glad to have somewhere to send it," he said, returning to his task, "because, for one thing, I'll have to use this office while I'm here."

"Oh?"

"I plan to stick around until the kids get adjusted. Keep my trips to a minimum."

"Well, that's what I…" She paused, taking a deep breath. He hadn't asked for her advice, but she had to say this. "I don't think it's a good idea to hire anyone from the Alston Agency."

"Oh?" She heard the none-of-your-business intonation in his voice and stiffened.

"They're just baby-sitters," she pressed on. "You need more of an all-around person. Now, Mrs. Fisher has a sister who, so she says, is very good with children, and a hard worker as well."

"Thank you." He kicked aside a box and turned to face her. "I have already hired Mrs. Johnson, whom the agency recommended very highly. I'd credit the word of a reputable agency against the word of somebody's sister anytime."

"Excuse me. It was just a suggestion." She held her back very erect as she walked out.

Officious! Too damned officious. When she can spare the time, that is, from her "gentlemen callers." The guy from the office—Gerald, wasn't it?—and now Horn Rims, and Lord knew how many others.

That bother you?

Hell, no! Just don't like her meddling. I knew it was a mistake moving here.

Proved to be convenient, didn't it?

Too damned convenient—for her!

But she did work fast. You get the kids tomorrow.

That's her job.

Not her job to clean up the place and dispose of all those things.

Doesn't give her the right to run my life.

Does it give you the right to act like a jerk?

Oh, hell!

There was no answer when he rang. But he knew she was in. He could hear a racket, a creaking, almost rhythmic sound. He pounded on the door.

"Come in," she called. "It's unlocked."

She had one of those minitrampolines in the middle of the floor and was rapidly jumping up and down on it. She didn't stop. Only gave him an "Oh, it's you" look.

"You shouldn't leave your door unlocked," he said. "Anybody could walk in."

"You're absolutely right about that." He could hardly mistake her meaning.

"Listen," he said. "I didn't mean to snap at you. I've just been a little uptight. Getting ready for the kids and all."

She didn't answer, just kept bouncing like a jumping jack.

"Damn it! Will you keep still! I'm trying to apologize."

"Unnecessary." She executed a swift half turn and increased her speed. He walked around to face her.

"Hey, cut out these crazy gymnastics and listen to me!"

"I suppose," she gasped, panting a little from her exercise, "that people only jump when you tell them to."

"You're absolutely right about that!" he mimicked, catching her in midair, and setting her down with her feet firmly planted on the solid floor. "Now just keep still a blasted minute! I'm trying to ask you out to dinner. Tonight. To celebrate the kids' coming home tomorrow."

"My, my! Such a gracious invitation!" Her eyes were blue thunderclouds and he was quite mesmerized by them, until he heard her next words. "It really pains me to decline. But I have another engagement tonight."

"That doesn't surprise me. I rather suspected you would."

"Now just what do you mean by that?" she snapped.

"Oh, never mind!" He strode out rapidly, slamming the door behind him.

CHAPTER SEVEN

SHE WAS NOT, Marcy decided, going to let Steve's animosity come between herself and the children. The adjustment they were making was crucial, and the main reason she'd wanted them near her was to help them through it.

"Your uncle Steve loves you," she told them. "That's why he wants you to live with him. So he can take care of you. And isn't it nice of him to bring you back to your own home, so you can go back to your old school and see your friends?"

The week he'd brought the children home, Steve arranged a memorial service for David and Diane, whose bodies had never been recovered after the accident. It was a short ceremony, a simple and moving tribute that brought Marcy to the brink of tears. Besides Steve and the children, only she and a few other friends and neighbors were present. The children sat quietly throughout the service, their faces solemn.

Afterward, Marcy felt that the memorial service had been a wise and necessary step, one that allowed all of them to come to terms with what had happened and to say a final goodbye to David and Diane.

The children were settling into a routine now, a routine that in many ways was a continuation of the past. Marcy kept her door open to them as she always had, with jigsaw puzzles and coloring books in the usual place at the bottom of her buffet. She also continued to take them out for little excursions. Steve did not object to this. In fact, he did not object to anything that made the children happy. He was too anxious to please them, Marcy thought; he couldn't deny them anything. If, once in a while, he did manage a not-too-firm "no," all Ginger had to do was cloud up and wail that she wanted her mommy and Steve would instantly succumb.

His attitude toward the children was so out-of-character, she thought. Once when she'd gone in to pick up the children she heard Steve in his office, evidently on the phone to someone in New York. He was barking out orders in a manner that left no doubt that whoever was on the other end of the line would hop to his bidding. Why didn't he just once bark at the kids? Didn't he know that children needed discipline? He was spoiling them rotten. But, of course, he'd never listen to her; he had to do everything his own way.

If he weren't so bullheaded, she would have felt sorry for him. Not only was he desperately trying to please two small children, he was also forced to cope with a household that revolved around their needs. Each evening when Marcy arrived home, she noticed Mrs. Johnson leaving. So, evidently, the housekeeper was not spending the night, and Marcy suspected she wasn't much help even while she was there.

Her suspicions were confirmed one Saturday in the laundry room. Marcy was just taking her towels out of the dryer when Steve came in carrying two pillowcases full of dirty clothes. He looked a bit harried, but he was whistling a tune under his breath, and when he saw her he smiled and nodded. Davey and Ginger, who were with him, immediately dashed over to her.

"Marcy!" Davey cried, "can we go to Funland tomorrow, or has the bank still got no money?"

"Well, er, we'll see." Marcy shot a quick glance at Steve, hoping he hadn't heard—or had, at least, misunderstood—Davey's reference to the day the automatic teller had registered Overdrawn. He was sorting clothes and putting them into two máchines and gave no indication that he'd heard. She quickly drew Davey's attention to another subject. "Here, come help me fold the towels."

"No, Ginger, you get your own," Davey admonished as he began to fold one. "I'm doing this by myself!"

"But I want to help," Ginger whined.

"All right, kids," Marcy broke in before Davey could refuse, "you take one end and let Ginger take the other. Then you'll get it done twice as fast." She was relieved that she'd been able to divert them from the automatic teller incident. Their romp in the park had turned out to be just as enjoyable as the rides at Funland would have been. Besides, her overdrawn bank account was certainly no business of the arrogant Mr. Prescott.

Ho! Ho! Ho! So Miss Efficiency Wilson has areas of inefficiency, Steve gloated as he stuffed a pair of Davey's jeans in with the dark clothes. Can't keep her bank account straight, huh? He wondered why the thought pleased him so much.

"Why are you smiling?" Marcy asked. "You like doing the laundry?"

"Oh! Er, I don't mind. I've done it before."

"Not for a long time, I bet," Marcy said, as she placed the last of her towels in the basket and thanked the children for their help.

"Well," he answered, "it's like riding a bicycle. You don't forget."

Davey ran up to them. "Can I have—?"

"Excuse me, please," Marcy said gently.

"'Scuse, please. I need money for a Popsicle, Steve."

Steve started to reach into his pocket, but Marcy intervened. "May I please have money for a Popsicle?" she prompted.

"May I, please?" asked Davey.

"Please," said Ginger. "Me too."

"Have you had your dinner?" Marcy asked, and when both children shook their heads, said, "Then the answer is *no*. Stay away from the vending machines and count the washing machines. Can you count them for me?"

Davey nodded and went off, counting loudly, with Ginger following.

Steve scowled at Marcy. "I thought they asked *me* for Popsicles."

"Somebody has to say no," she answered, unperturbed. "You spoil them. You must be spoiling Mrs. Johnson, too. Doesn't she do the wash?"

"Alston Agency rules." Steve's mouth tightened as he poured the soap in and started the machines. "She doesn't do wash. She doesn't do cleaning. She doesn't do cooking. She baby-sits."

"From what I can see, she doesn't do much of that," Marcy said. "The kids are in school half the day, and I see her leaving at five. Doesn't she stay overnight?"

"If I pay her overtime." Steve frowned as he dusted soap powder from his hands. "Which I don't mind, but it galls the hell out of me to cook her breakfast the next morning."

"Oh. I see." Marcy's eyes twinkled, and he could tell it was all she could do to keep from laughing. The return of the children, just then, served as a momentary distraction.

"Ten, Marcy. I counted ten machines," Davey burst out.

"Me too," said Ginger.

"Ten! Aren't you smart? Listen, can you hop on one foot like this?" She demonstrated.

"Oh, sure," Davey said.

"Me too," came the echo.

"All right. Try it. Count how many times on one foot." She turned back to Steve as the children went off, happily counting. "Watch out! You might be in the breadline soon. Because if you run your business the way you run your household—"

"Okay. Okay. I've already given the woman notice. But I never had to do all this before. I lived in a hotel and went out for my meals or—"

"Change of life-style, huh?" Marcy teased, as she began to retrieve her lingerie from the gentle-dry cycle.

"All right. Your point has been made. You don't have to rub my nose in it."

"Why, Steve Prescott, I never once said 'I told you so.'"

"No. That's right. You didn't." He watched her shaking out a frilly piece of nightwear that looked as if it belonged to a very seductive woman, though in those jeans she seemed as young and slender as a child. There was obviously more to Marcy Wilson than met the eye....

"Well, happy laundering," Marcy said as she picked up her basket.

"Hey, wait!" His mind had wandered so far afield that he'd almost forgotten to ask, "Look, will you kindly lead me to somebody's sister who does do wash?"

"Fifteen times, Marcy," Davey chimed in, "I hopped fifteen times."

"Me too," said Ginger.

"She did not," Davey scoffed. "She just hopped nine."

"That's great." Marcy put down her basket and bent to hug both children. "Now try it on the other foot." As they began to hop and count, she again picked up her basket of clothes. "I'll see if she's still available," she told Steve as she went out.

"Thanks. I'd appreciate that," he called, hating to see her go. She sure knows how to handle the kids, he thought. They never minded when she said no. They just went off hopping and counting and laughing. He smiled to himself. Laughing. That was it, she made them laugh. Marcy was so lively and yet there was a warmth about her. Yes, he admitted, there was something special about Marcy Wilson, something alluring and... Oh Lord, he'd better keep his distance.

Marcy did manage to engage the cleaning woman's sister for him. Sally Chisholm was buxom and cheerful—"a real jewel," as he described her to Marcy. Beds got made, meals cooked, and the children were brought under control.

"You're too soft with them," Mrs. Chisholm had immediately told Steve. "You've got to let them know you're the boss, Mr. Prescott."

Steve appreciated the order she brought to his household and he was grateful to Marcy for finding her. However, he did not renew his invitation to take her out to dinner. Instead, he brought her a gift the next time he returned from New York. A Rolex watch. It seemed that was what all the ladies wanted.

When he gave it to her, she stared at it, then looked up at him, her eyes expressing a strange combination of surprise, pleasure and denial.

"Oh, you shouldn't! This is too much!"

"Just a little token to say thanks for all the help." He could hardly speak. Her eyes were casting a strange spell over him, and her lips were parted, an invitation he found hard to resist.

"But I didn't . . . I mean, I only helped because I wanted to."

"I know. You did it for Diane." He tore his gaze from that provocative face and concentrated on extracting the watch from the box. "Here. Let's see how it looks on your wrist." He slipped the watch over her hand, but was so moved by the feel of her soft smooth skin against his fingers that he quickly withdrew. "Wear it for Diane. We both thank you." He hurried out before she could make any more protest. And before he was tempted to do more than he should.

MRS. CHISHOLM was never able to stay overnight. "Not when you have half-grown children like I have, Mr. P. I don't mind being away during the day while they're in school. But at night I have to be there to check on their comings and goings. Now, there's my oldest, Nance. She'll be eighteen next month, and she's pretty reliable. I could bring her to stay overnight whenever you're away.''

He did make one two-day trip to New York, accepting this arrangement. Everything went well. Anyway, the current situation was only temporary. He had a real-estate agent searching for a small country place in either Connecticut or upstate New York. The kids could have their ponies, and commuting would certainly be easier than from California. If he bought such a place he'd have to hire an adequate staff, of course, but his main worry was to find a woman who could take care of the children and manage the household, as well. His secretary had suggested a nanny for the children and a butler for the household. Steve couldn't help grinning when she said it. A butler? Such a grandiose arrangement had never occurred to him. But, what the hell! He had the money. Whatever the children needed, the children would get.

Meanwhile he struggled with the situation as it was. The children seemed happy with Mrs. Chisholm and their school. He was straightening out their financial and legal affairs, and he didn't plan to make any long trips until the family was permanently settled.

One morning at six, his partner phoned. ''Steve, we've got problems.''

''Oh?'' Steve stifled a yawn and tried to concentrate.

''Peru. There's a hitch about the claims. Holding up everything. You'd better get down there.''

''I thought Stan was handling it.''

''Oh, hell!'' Brick shouted. ''You know Stan and the way he fumbles. Anyway, it's your baby.''

''Don't see how I can make it, Brick. I don't like to leave the kids. I don't want to leave them until—''

''You think you've got troubles!'' Brick bellowed. ''All hell's breaking loose up here. Stell's on the rampage. Trying to take me to the cleaners—wants my money and her new guy too! And somebody's got to be here to handle those options on the Saudi Arabia claims, which, I'd like to remind you, is also your baby. Anyway, it'd only take you a week to get things going again. Stan could carry on after that."

A week. Only a week.

"Okay. I guess I can arrange it." Mrs. Chisholm was running the household anyway, and her daughter could stay nights. He would ask Marcy to keep an eye on things.

But when he went next door to talk to Marcy, he saw her going down the steps with Horn Rims. They were holding hands. He felt a sudden sense of loneliness—as if he'd somehow been abandoned. Oh, hell! he thought with sudden anger. What was he thinking of? He didn't need her to look after anything!

ON THURSDAY AFTERNOON, Marcy was able to return Troy to his mother, who had completely recovered from her surgery and was back at work. She was so pleased with the excellent care Troy had received and so grateful for Marcy's help that she invited her to stay for tea and cookies. Marcy didn't get home until almost seven and when she entered the apartment, the phone was ringing. It was Gerald.

"Marcy, would you please come to the hospital? I'm in Emergency."

"Emergency!" Marcy exclaimed. "What's wrong? Are you—?"

"It's not me. It's Pop. And I don't know what's wrong. He'd passed out and was lying on the floor when I got home. I was late because I stopped for a beer. I should have come straight home. Marcy, I'm scared!"

"I'll be right there," she said. When she arrived at the hospital, Mr. Sims had already been taken to intensive care. Gerald was waiting for Marcy, and the two of them went up together.

"They think it's his heart," Gerald said. He was visibly distressed, and Marcy sat with him in the waiting area for several hours, until the doctor came out to announce that Mr. Sims's condition had stabilized. They were running tests to determine the extent of the damage. There would almost certainly be no change until morning, he told them, suggesting they go home and wait.

Marcy could see that Gerald needed food and rest and urged him to come back to her place. When they got there, however, he said he wasn't hungry.

"Well, I am," Marcy told him emphatically. "I'll fix us something light. One good thing about being extravagant is that you're always prepared." As she spoke, she took a carton of fresh oysters from the refrigerator.

After a bowl of hot oyster stew and a glass of wine, Gerald said he felt much refreshed and would go back to the hospital.

"You'll do no such thing," she insisted. "You left my number and they'll call if you're needed. Why don't you sleep here on the couch, and if they do call, I'll go back to the hospital with you." She set out sheets and blankets for him and placed the phone close by. When he declared he was "as snug as a bug in a rug," she got into her own bed and fell instantly asleep.

STEVE DIDN'T LIKE being away from the children a whole week. He had called as soon as he arrived in Peru, and things at home seemed to be going reasonably well. However, he'd been out in the field for two days because they'd had helicopter problems. It was almost three in the morning when he got back to the station, which meant that it was around midnight in California. But he had to leave for the site at six, when it would be three a.m., their time. Better call now, he decided.

The phone rang and rang. Nancy must be a heavy sleeper, he thought. He gripped the phone hard as he waited. Finally, it was picked up at the other end.

"Hello," said a sleepy little voice.

"Davey! Is that you, Davey?"

"Uh-huh," Davey said with a yawn.

"Why did you answer the phone?"

"It rang."

"Where's Nancy?" Steve felt a growing panic.

"Don't know. Sleeping, I guess."

"Davey, listen to me. You go wake her up and tell her to come to the phone."

"Okay."

Steve held the phone so tightly his knuckles whitened. Why the hell hadn't the Chisholm girl answered? The phone was right next to the bed. No, he thought, the tension easing a bit. She would probably be in the extra bed in Ginger's room, and maybe she hadn't—

"Hello," came Davey's voice.

"Where's Nancy?"

"She's not there."

"Not there! What do you mean? Did you look? Everywhere?"

"Yes. And I called her. I called and called. And Ginger woke up, and she's crying. And Nancy's not here."

Cold terror seized him. The girl wasn't there. The children were alone in the apartment. Now he had awakened them and . . .

"Listen, Davey, listen to me." He made an effort to speak calmly and clearly. "This is what I want you to do. You go. . . No. You and Ginger stay right there. Understand? I'm going to call Marcy. You wait."

Marcy's phone was answered on the first ring.

"Hello." A man's voice.

"Is this Miss Wilson's residence?"

"Yes, it is. Sims here. Did you want me?"

"What! Oh, no. No. I'd like to speak with Miss Wilson. Please."

"Oh. Sure. Just a minute."

Steve waited, fuming. Damn! He might have known she'd have some joker—

"Hello." Her voice sounded muffled, as if she'd just woken up. Under his panic lurked a disquieting thought. Something he'd have to deal with later. Now his concern was for the children.

"Marcy, this is Steve. I'm in Peru, and the children are alone in the apartment."

"What!"

"That girl—Nancy, Mrs. Chisholm's daughter. She's supposed to be staying with them, but Davey says she's not there, and I . . . Marcy, would you—?"

"All right, Steve. I'll go right over."

"I'll give you ten minutes, then I'll call back."

"All right. I'm off," she said.

When he called his apartment again Marcy answered.

"The kids are fine. And don't worry. I'll stay with them. Tonight, and every night until you get back."

"Thank you," Steve said. The relief that flooded through him was overwhelming. With Marcy he knew the children would be safe.

Then the disquieting thought he had earlier shrugged aside returned. Marcy's phone had been answered by a man, a man who assumed the call was for him. And obviously, both the man and Marcy had been asleep.

That bother you?

Hell, no! Why should it?

NANCY TOLD MARCY that she'd just gone out for a few minutes with her boyfriend to get a hamburger. The children were asleep, and anyway, they'd come right back, and would Marcy please not tell her mother what had happened. So Marcy simply told Mrs. Chisholm that Steve had asked her to stay at night, so Nancy would not be needed.

Mrs. Chisholm said that was fine, as she really wanted Nancy at home where she could keep her eye on her "comings and goings."

"Poor Mr. Prescott," Mrs. Chisholm continued. "He just doesn't know what to do with these children. They lead him around by the nose. He needs to get married, and I don't doubt he will soon, the way these women are after him. All the letters he gets. Of course, I never open them, but I can smell the perfume right through the envelopes. Like they just poured it on, so he wouldn't forget. And some woman keeps calling him on the phone. I think she's the one in the photograph I set up on his dresser. Isn't she a beauty?"

She was a beauty. Long blond hair and a wide mouth curved in a provocative smile. And a scribbled autograph, "To my darling Steve, with all my love, Tricia."

Yes, Marcy told Mrs. Chisholm, he probably would marry soon. And yes, it would be a good thing. And the only reason she was upset, she told herself, was that someone else would be a mother to Ginger and Davey.

Although Mrs. Chisholm's position had been a temporary arrangement, Steve gave her a sizable bonus when his secretary found a Mrs. Evans, who had good references and no encumbrances. He turned the office into a bedroom and had Mrs. Evans flown out to occupy it. Although she lacked Mrs. Chisholm's warmth, she was efficient, reliable and . . . well, almost suitable.

"ROB PETER . . . pay Paul. Rob Peter . . . pay Paul," Ginger sang from her seat on the floor while she tried unsuccessfully to braid the yellow yarn that was Lilli Ann's hair.

"A new nursery song?" Steve asked, looking up from his newspaper.

Ginger shook her head and Davey replied. "It's not a song. It's what Marcy says—'Can't play now. I got to rob Peter to pay Paul,'" he mimicked, then looked seriously at Steve. "She's not really robbing. She's not a bad guy."

"Oh?"

"Marcy told me. She's not robbing. She's just making her money go round and round." Davey waved his arms dramatically before returning to his book. But Steve could not return to his newspaper.

Making her money go round and round? He knew Marcy worked hard. How much were they paying her? He stirred in his chair, not amused as he'd been earlier, when he heard about the overdrawn bank account. Somehow he didn't like to think of Marcy being pinched to make ends meet. She didn't give that impression; she dressed well, glowed with health, always looked cheerful. Wouldn't even take the cleaning money he'd given her.

Because she was a *giver*. Not a *taker*. Whenever he needed her, Marcy had come through. And not only had he not reciprocated, he'd avoided her like the plague. He'd never even taken her out to dinner. Well . . . that was because he didn't want to get involved.

Taking a lady out to dinner has never involved you yet. Right!

He put down his newspaper and stood up to go next door.

CHAPTER EIGHT

HER DINING TABLE was littered with bills, so she must have been busy trying to make her money go "round and round." Evidently she was ready to give up the effort, for she said she'd be delighted to go to dinner with him. He took her to The Captain's Table.

"I'm glad you chose this place. I love it." She looked up from her salad at the hurricane lamps set in sconces in the wall and the antique map of the New World. "Don't you feel you're on board an old ship sailing off to some unknown faraway place?"

"Not really," he said. "I get the impression I'm on an old paddle wheeler that's been converted into a rather luxurious restaurant and docked on the banks of the Sacramento River."

"Oh." She gave him a pitying look. "Must you be so realistic? All right. Try this. Just let yourself go. Feel the gentle rocking of the boat. It *is* rocking—don't you feel it?" He nodded, smiling, and she went on. "Hear the waves lapping against the hull and watch the lights of the other craft as they sail by. Look!"

Their table was by the window, and he could see the lights of a couple of boats that were sailing by.

"Now, just relax," she told him in a coaxing tone. "You're sailing down the Mississippi on a brand-new paddle wheeler—a freshly painted, well-appointed showboat. You've just come from the gaming table after a big win, and you're having dinner with—"

"Then why," he asked, laughing, "do I still feel I'm in a restaurant on an old paddle wheeler that's been—"

"That's only because you have no imagination!" She leaned toward him, her eyes dancing with mischief. "Would you believe you were on a showboat if I sat on top of that piano and sang 'Can't Help Lovin' That Man of Mine'?"

"I dare you," he said with a chuckle, rather enjoying this silly game she was playing. Come to think of it, she was always playing games. She turned disciplining the children into fun. And, yes, even her money problems. What did she call it...robbing Peter to pay Paul? She makes a game of life, he thought, and smiled.

"You needn't smile like that. I'm not going to take you up on your dare. It wouldn't spur your imagination, and I'd just be making a spectacle of myself."

"Not you. You could never be a spectacle. You'd be a vision—a beautiful vision." The words came out almost involuntarily, for that was exactly what he was thinking. She *was* a vision, in a simple shirtwaist dress of lavender silk that gave her blue eyes a violet cast. Her peal of laughter delighted him, as it always did.

Marcy's eyes widened. "Your imagination is operative after all! If you can picture me as a beautiful vision, you might even acquire the visualization technique."

"Visualization? You mean seeing what's before you?"

"No. It's seeing what's *not* before you," she said, as she took a sip of wine. "I read this book—can't remember the title—it describes a technique for getting what you want or bringing about what you wish would happen. You just pretend it's already happened, and you keep seeing it in your mind and it comes true. Do you believe that?"

"No," he said. "I do not believe that." How many times with childlike faith had he envisioned his mother coming home? All the nights he'd lulled himself to sleep feeling in his mind her hugs and kisses as he imagined her return. It had never happened.

"No," he repeated. "I definitely do not believe that."

"I'm not convinced myself," she agreed, as the waiter removed their salad plates and placed the entrées before them. When he had departed, she began to eat with relish, and smiled across at Steve.

"I'm glad I'm with you."

"Oh?" He felt strangely pleased.

"Because—" she paused with a dainty morsel halfway to her mouth "—I love lobster, and you can afford it."

"And I thought it was my manly charm." He chuckled, amused by her frankness. "Tell me, do you make your selection from the menu with a view to your escort's pocketbook?"

"Yes, indeed. My brother, Bill, says it's definitely the polite thing to do." Then she added teasingly, "I'm not sure about your charm, but you have a very nice smile."

"Thank you," he said, rather absently. He was thinking of Horn Rims, who drove a Mercedes. "Then do you choose..." He broke off. He couldn't ask that.

"The answer to your unspoken question," she said calmly, "is no. I do not choose my escorts according to what's in their pockets. I like hamburgers, too. In other words—" she gave a dramatic wave of her hand "—king or commoner, it's all the same to me."

"No preferences?" he asked. *In food or men?*

"Variety is the spice of life. This lobster is delicious." She speared a piece and held it toward him. "Would you like a taste?"

"No!" he snapped, angry that he could not stop looking at her. He wanted to kiss her. He wanted to shake her. He wanted to ask her what the hell Gerald Sims was doing asleep at her place in the middle of the night. No! He didn't want to know.

"My goodness, don't look like that! You don't have to taste the lobster if you don't want to. I'm not forcing it on you. But you've hardly touched your steak. Aren't you hungry?''

"Er..." He tore his gaze from her, and looked down at his wineglass, turning it slowly. "I was thinking of something else.''

"Yes," she said. "I suppose you must have a lot on your mind. Is the new housekeeper working out all right?''

"Huh? Oh, yeah, so far so good." At that moment, Mrs. Evans was the farthest thing from his mind. "I—I want to thank you again for coming to my rescue that night.''

"Oh, I'm just glad I was there. I was as concerned as you.''

"I know. But it was a bad time for you. I hated to disturb you so late.''

She shrugged. "No problem.''

"I know you had company. The, er, man who answered the phone seemed a little put out." He watched for her reaction.

"Gerald? Oh, no," she said, as she lifted her glass. "It was just that he was waiting for a call.''

"He's in the habit of getting calls at your place in the middle of the night?" He could not help blurting it out any more than he could stop the hot blood rushing to his face.

She put down her fork and looked at him. "You're asking if Gerald is in the habit of spending the night at my place?''

"Oh, no. That's not my business.''

"It certainly isn't. However, to satisfy your obvious curiosity, on that particular night Gerald had just taken his father to Emergency. I realized he was extremely upset, and in case anything happened, I wanted to be able to go back to the hospital with him. So I suggested he spend the night at my place. On my sofa! When the phone rang at such a late hour, he naturally thought it was the hospital and—''

"All right. All right. I get the picture." His shame was coupled with overwhelming relief.

Why? What's it to you?

Nothing! It meant nothing to him.

"I . . . I'm sorry I asked. I didn't mean to give the impression that—"

"That you thought I was shacking up with any Tom, Dick or Harry that came along?"

"No, I didn't think that. I . . . look, don't be angry with me. Come on, finish your dinner."

She blinked several times. "I'm not angry. And I'm not hungry."

"Would you like a doggie bag?"

"No."

"Dessert? Coffee?"

"No, thanks. Oh, well, I'll have a cup of coffee while you finish your steak."

"Never mind." He pushed back his plate. "I'm not hungry, either. Let's go."

On the drive home, neither tried to engage the other in conversation. They were still silent when they left the car and walked toward the apartments.

"Thank you for a very nice evening," she said politely, as she reached into her purse for the key. He took it from her, opened the door and followed her in.

"I had a nice evening," he said. "I'm sorry it had to end this way. Sorry that what I said made you angry. And don't tell me again that you're not angry."

"But I'm not—" She broke off, then tossed her coat and purse on the sofa and turned to face him. "It wasn't what you said. It was what you implied."

"I didn't imply anything," he argued, aware that this was not exactly the truth. Aware of how desirable she looked in that simple little dress.

"Yes, you did. You have a one-track mind. You think the only thing that can exist between a man and a woman is sex. And that really bugs me. Haven't you ever heard of good old-fashioned friendship?"

"Of course."

"But you don't think of it between a man and a woman, do you? Like most men, you look at a woman in terms of her sexual attractiveness."

"You find that offensive? As lovely as you are?"

"I don't find it offensive, but I just think—"

"Then you shouldn't find this offensive, either." He did what he'd been wanting to do all evening. He took her in his arms. For a moment he just held her cradled against his chest, his face buried in her hair, savoring the sweet fresh fragrance.

"I'm sorry I said something to hurt you," he whispered. "I . . . I thought . . . I was so . . ." He broke off. He couldn't say he was jealous. He wasn't jealous! Lord, she was sweet. He traced light kisses over her temple and closed eyelids. Then his lips brushed hers, slowly, tentatively. Her mouth felt soft and warm against his, and the kiss deepened as she wound her arms around him and pressed closer.

Wild desire churned within him. He wanted this woman. He wanted to hold her. To love her. But somewhere deep in his consciousness an alarm had sounded. This was more than passion. Instinctively he felt that her warm and trusting response was answering more than the urgency of the moment. She was drawing him into the future.

Abruptly he released her, backing away from his own desire and the puzzled question in her eyes.

"I'm sorry," he said. "I shouldn't have done that."

She started to protest, and he turned quickly away. "I'd better end the evening before I find myself having to make more apologies. Good night."

Back in his own place, he took a cold shower, muttering, cursing to himself. He should never have taken her out, never have kissed her. He had sensed from the first that Marcy was a woman from whom he could not easily walk away. And he wanted no woman he couldn't walk away from. His mother's desertion had turned his father into a bitter angry man. Steve had hated him; he hadn't realized until it was too late that his father was hurting, too.

You couldn't trust a woman. Any woman. He thought of that guy he'd worked with down in Mexico—Scully, Sam Scully. Tough guy. You'd never have believed he'd go off the deep end the way he did. They were out in the field, and someone brought in the mail. And Sam got that "Dear John" letter from his wife. And he'd just walked out and shot himself.... And Stell and Brick—crazy in love last year, and now she'd dumped him for another guy and they were fighting like cats and dogs over the kid and the money.

He shook his head as he toweled himself dry. This was a love 'em and leave 'em world, and he wanted no part of it. He'd vowed a long time ago that he'd never fall in love, never marry. He knew that if he were to keep his vow, he'd better stay away from Marcy. Stick to a woman like Trish, who warmed his bed, but not his heart.

CHAPTER NINE

SHE'D BEEN KISSED before. But never had anyone apologized for kissing her. Marcy leaned against the closed door, feeling the humiliation of his rejection. He had practically pushed her away!

Face it, Marcy! He *had* to push you away. You were clinging to him like crazy, virtually inviting him to...

Oh, no! It wasn't like that. It wasn't! Marcy pressed her burning face against the cool panel of the door. It had seemed so natural. The warmth of his arms had been so male, so confident, that she had melted against him. She had sensed a gentle tenderness in him and sensed, too, a passion, an urgency that shattered her every reserve. She had pressed closer, yielding to some primitive desire that clamored to be fulfilled. And he had pushed her away.

She felt a hot flush of anger. You initiated that kiss, Mr. Prescott! And if you think I'm going to spend half the night mooning over it, you're crazy! I'm not Jennifer.

Marcy snatched her coat from the sofa and marched resolutely upstairs. Jennifer. Lord, how she had mooned over Al. Jennifer had practically cried in her soup last week, when they'd played tennis and had lunch together. The whole conversation had centered on Al. His frequent business trips, his golf and how little time he spent with her. Jennifer had sounded so unhappy and unsure, almost as she had in the days before her marriage, when she used to wonder if Al really loved her. Now Marcy was beginning to understand the reason for her sister's depression. It was more than boredom, she realized. Jennifer had become dependent on Al and that dependency made her vulnerable.

Well, it won't happen to me, Marcy promised herself as she vigorously brushed her hair. I'm not going to moon over anyone. So you can spread your smiles and your kisses around just as you please, Mr. Prescott. It won't bother me.

Suddenly she stopped, the brush held in midair. *He* had pulled away. He wasn't spreading his kisses around. Saving them for his true love? The blonde in the silver frame? Well, that didn't bother her, either. She ignored the little ache in the pit of her stomach and eventually fell asleep dreaming of a man whose eyes crinkled when he smiled.

"DON'T YOU LOVE US anymore, Marcy?"

"Of course I love you," Marcy answered, as she scooped Ginger up into her arms.

"How much? How much?" The little girl giggled. It was an old game.

"A bushel and a peck, and a hug around the neck." Marcy gave her a hug, then put her down and sank to her knees beside Davey. She felt a little breathless. The day was mild for early November, and Marcy had jogged through the park, approaching the complex from the rear and coming upon the children playing outside. She pulled gently at Davey's ear and gave him a kiss on the cheek.

"I love you, too," she said. "What are you doing?"

"Making a mountain," he answered, never pausing as he raked leaves into a pile with his hands. "Where have you been, Marcy?"

"I've been visiting a friend who's just come home from the hospital. I'm teaching him to play chess." Gerald's father had had a coronary bypass, and was recuperating at home.

"Why don't you play with us anymore?" asked Ginger.

"Well...you've been busy at school, and I've been busy at work." She couldn't tell the children that she had to avoid them in order to avoid their uncle. "And I'm playing with you now," she said, adding a few leaves to Davey's pile.

"My teacher says it's almost Thanksgiving. Is it, Marcy?" Davey asked.

"It will be in a week or so."

"And that's when we're going?" Davey's eyes were eager.

"Going?"

"You know. To 'silomar."

"Oh." That conference at Asilomar. She'd forgotten about it. But Lord, kids never forgot anything.

"You said you were going to take us. You promised," said Davey.

"Me too," echoed Ginger.

"Well, now, I don't know. You see, I'd have to ask your Uncle Steve."

"Well, there he is." Davey pointed excitedly. "Ask him now, Marcy."

Steve had been standing on the balcony observing the little group for some time. Mrs. Evans had asked him to call the children to dinner, and he'd stepped out, looking over the railing.

He'd noticed her immediately. She was wearing a vivid green running suit with a hood. The hood had fallen back, and her hair was blowing in the breeze as she sat in the middle of those leaves, laughing. It was as if the day had brightened as he watched her. She looked so alive as she played with the children. And they accepted her so easily and naturally.

He felt a wave of envy. With him, the children were still awkward and ill at ease. He had tried so hard... "How was school today, Davey?" And Davey would answer in a monosyllable and retreat to his own room or as far from Steve as he could. Ginger would trail after her brother. He felt as though he were walking on eggs, trying to please them, trying to get close to them. But he hadn't managed to

make even a dent in their affections. He wanted them to love
him, more for their sake than for his own. How could they
be happy, living with a stranger? He kept telling himself it
would take time, but—

"Ask him! Ask him!" he heard Davey shout.

"Ask me what?" he called good-naturedly, smiling as he
gazed down at them, desperately wanting to be a part of
their easy camaraderie.

Marcy looked up reluctantly. And she was immediately
arrested by that smile and reminded of that kiss. She
flushed, remembering his rejection, and felt too confused to
respond to Davey's request. When she didn't speak, Davey
supplied the question himself.

"Marcy was going to take us to 'silomar. She already
promised and everything. Only now she says she has to ask
you. Can we? Can we go?"

Steve frowned, and Marcy sensed his irritation.

"I've never stopped you from going anywhere with
Marcy. She can take you wherever she wants."

His answer satisfied the children, who began to jump up
and down with glee. Marcy felt compelled to explain that
they were talking about a five-day trip, which had been
planned several months before.

"So come in and tell me about it," Steve said. "Mrs. Evans has chili waiting. There's plenty. Join us, Marcy, and we
can talk about it."

Marcy joined them because . . . well, because she'd promised the children and she'd have to clear it with him first.
And, she told herself, you don't have to avoid a man just to
keep from falling in love with him! Anyway, she was hungry.

Over a really delicious bowl of hot chili, she explained the
plans she'd made with David and Diane. During Thanksgiving week, Marcy was to take the children with her to Asilomar, where she'd be conducting a couple of workshops at
a parenting conference. There would be other children, too,

and programs had been arranged for them, as well as for the parents.

"It might be good for Ginger and Davey to get away for a while," she said, "and it would be a break for you."

Steve seemed very interested in the conference and plied her with questions. She described the various sessions that were designed to help foster parents in the care and guidance of children.

"This conference. Can anybody go?" he asked.

"Why, yes," she said, surprised at the eagerness in his voice. "They're primarily for foster parents, but they are open to the general public."

"Have they found it helpful? I mean these people who attend—do they really get something out of it?"

She hesitated. "Well, those who come intending to get something out of it usually do. So I guess the answer is yes. Otherwise, we would have discontinued it altogether."

"Then I think it's a good idea for the kids. And for me, too. Where do I register?"

"You?" Marcy asked, feeling a little stunned.

"Why are you looking at me like that? I thought you'd be the first to say I need a few lessons in parenting."

SHE HAD NOT BELIEVED he'd follow through, but he did. He even suggested they take his car, since they were all going and surely couldn't fit into her Volkswagen.

"What kind of car do you have in New York?" she asked, as they started out in the modest Chevrolet, the rental car he had driven since arriving in California.

"I don't own a car," he said. "Matter of fact, I've never owned one."

"Oh?"

"Well, by the time I got so I could afford one, I was either in some godforsaken place where we travel by helicopter or in New York where it's easier to take a cab."

"I see." She looked at his hands, firm on the wheel, and noted his relaxed manner as he drove onto the freeway. "You drive as if you've been doing it for a long time."

"I did a lot of driving when I was in the navy. They stuck me in the motor pool right away. Good thing I did a driver's ed course in high school that last year I was home." He took a deep breath. "Funny. I wanted a car like crazy then. I thought for sure that by the time I was sixteen, I . . . Well, it didn't work out."

"Most kids want a car at that age, but very few get it," she said, wanting to chase that bitter look from his face.

"Right." The single word was like the sound of a door shutting, closing off the past. Marcy realized how little she knew about this man. How much she wanted to know.

"When did you join the navy?" she prompted.

"A few months past my sixteenth birthday."

"Sixteen!"

He grinned. "Well, I lied a little. I was on my own and jobs were scarce, so I joined the navy to see the world." He chuckled. "Never got off the base."

Marcy was eager to hear more about his stint in the navy and what he'd done after that. But they were interrupted by a minor squabble in the back seat. Ginger had torn Davey's comic book. Marcy pulled out the coloring books and crayons she'd brought, and when the children were quiet again, she turned back to Steve.

"Did you get anything out of the navy besides a special aptitude for driving a car?"

"Well, yes." He smiled as he gave her a sidelong glance. "I had to take the G.E.D.—you know, that high-school equivalency test, so I guess I got my high-school diploma. And I met Brick." He said that Brick's father had always worked in the oil fields, and Brick had plenty of ideas. So when they got their discharge papers, the two of them teamed up. They started off doing drudge work in the fields, eventually turned to speculation, then formed a partnership and . . .

"Well, we've been pretty lucky," he concluded.

"You must have worked really hard. And you made it on your own. I think you can be pretty proud of yourself." She touched his hand and flashed him a brilliant smile. She didn't add that she thought there was something pretty special about a man who could afford any kind of car he wanted, yet felt comfortable and content driving a modest rental Chevy. Her brother, Bill, who couldn't afford it, and Tom Jenkins, who could, drove only what was flashy, foreign and very expensive.

Marcy watched Steve as he calmly negotiated the heavy Sunday afternoon traffic, and imagined a skinny underage kid deftly handling the trucks and jeeps in a navy motor pool. She saw a man in dingy overalls digging or doing whatever they did in oil fields. She heard a stranger say, "I'll be there to pick them up." She saw a man with a sweet smile stuffing kids' clothes into a washing machine. This was a man who did whatever he had to do, no matter how unfamiliar or difficult. Marcy felt an overwhelming rush of tenderness toward him. She wanted to put her arms around him, lean her head against his shoulder and say, "I think you're great!" Then she remembered. This was a man who did not want to be touched.

"You know," he said, startling her out of her reverie, "I've traveled practically all over the world, but very little in the United States, and not at all in California."

"You're going to love this place. Someone—I think it was Hemingway—called the Pacific Grove area the most beautiful spot in the world."

When they arrived, she could tell he was impressed by the conference grounds at Asilomar, where much of the rustic beauty had been retained. The main buildings and guest cottages, with names like Crescent View, Fireside and Seaside, were scattered among towering trees. At the end of the grounds, sandy dunes led to a picturesque and very rocky beach. Marcy and Steve were housed in adjoining cottages, Marcy sharing her room with Ginger, and Davey staying with Steve.

Because the other conference participants weren't scheduled to arrive until three, the next afternoon, Marcy said the four of them would spend the whole day together and take the grand tour. They set out Monday after breakfast in a lighthearted holiday mood. First, they followed the famous seventeen-mile drive with its beautiful views: the great Pacific Ocean with the waves rushing in, breaking upon the rocks and the windswept beach, the gnarled and twisted cypress trees that bent inland, as if losing the battle against the wind and sea. From time to time, they caught glimpses of luxurious houses, nestled in the hills.

They drove into Monterey and ate at the Carousel, where the children consumed hot dogs and milk shakes and took several rides on the indoor carousel, and where Steve, between mouthfuls of homemade peach cobbler and mounds of ice cream, remarked that it was a shame to place a honky-tonk town in the midst of such natural beauty.

However, he was impressed by the aquarium with its magnificent man-made fish tanks, tanks so huge one could walk around them and observe the different species of sea life that dwelt in Monterey Bay. They all agreed that they were lucky to arrive at feeding time. The children had enormous fun watching the sea otters swim up to catch their portions of fish. Ginger particularly enjoyed the touch tank, lifting out one and then another of the rubbery-looking starfish, which neither Marcy nor Davey would touch. Davey's favorite attraction was the simulated surf. He stood, watching the water gently recede, laughing each time the big wave formed and then surged out with such force that light sprays would come shooting out at him.

They returned to Asilomar contentedly weary, had dinner in the community dining hall and retired early.

The next two days were filled with the real work of the conference. Marcy conducted two workshops, both of which Steve attended. She was surprised by his conscientiousness and active participation. He also attended several other workshops. He's serious about parenting, Marcy thought—determined to be good at whatever he has to do. Again, she felt that rush of tenderness toward him.

Thanksgiving was a day for relaxing and having fun, with excursions in the morning, an early turkey dinner with all the trimmings and, in the afternoon, a social for the adults and supervised play for the children.

"I don't feel social," Steve said to Marcy. "Let's take a walk on the beach."

"I don't know," she said. "Maybe I should be around in case someone wants to talk to me or ask any questions."

"You've been answering questions for two days, teacher. It's time you took a rest. Come on." His hand firmly grasped hers and she had no choice but to follow.

The day was overcast and a little chilly, so they went back to the cottages and changed into warm running suits and sturdy shoes. A few minutes later, they were climbing through the sand dunes toward the beach.

"I feel like I'm playing hooky," she said, laughing. She did feel as carefree as a child let out of school. Climbing through the dunes was difficult, though. She kept slipping backward and would have fallen except for his supporting hand.

"I can see you're not used to roughing it," he said, and in one surprising movement, lifted her in his arms. Her own arms went automatically around his neck, and she felt the light stubble on his chin as it rested against her cheek. Her heart thumped wildly. She told herself it was from the effort of the climb, told herself that the heady exhilaration she felt was purely from the fresh sea air that was filling her lungs.

"Here we are," he said, as they reached level ground. He turned his face toward her as he spoke, and his lips almost brushed hers. She held her breath as his eyes searched hers for a long moment. She thought—hoped—that he was going to kiss her. She felt a wave of keen disappointment when he set her firmly on her feet.

"I'll race you to that rock," he said, pointing to a spot a good distance away from them.

She was glad to run, to let go, to feel the tension flow out of her. For a time they kept pace, but at the last minute he swiftly passed her. When she reached him, he was already standing on the rock, and he stretched down his hand to help her up.

It was a large flat rock, half on land, half in the water. Marcy sat, exhausted but composed, feeling a certain peace as she absorbed her surroundings. Except for the two of them, the beach was deserted. There were only the rocks, the wet sand and the rhythmic gray sea, rolling in, receding and rolling out again. Steve sat down beside her, and she felt as if they existed in a world apart.

"Now, isn't this better than standing around saying 'how do you do,' and 'how do you like the conference'?" he asked, as he tossed a stone into the water.

"Definitely," she answered. "And how *do* you like the conference, sir?"

"It's great! What I like most about it is listening to the foster parents themselves talk about how they handled this situation or that. They're a good group. This foster-parent system of yours is terrific."

"Not really. There are...many imperfections." When he looked at her in surprise, she added, "These people here are just the tip of the iceberg, or maybe I should say the cream of the crop. They're sincere, like you," she said, smiling. Then she frowned, and one slender hand made circles on the rock as she looked out to sea. "For every good one, there are ten others who are barely adequate."

"But you—the agency, I mean—is so thorough about selection and supervision. I should think—"

She turned a serious face toward him. "The average social worker has a caseload of between fifty and sixty children. When you consider that he or she has to counsel the children, the natural parents, if they're still around, as well as the foster parents, you can imagine how little time there is for each. And how hard it is to spot the bad ones."

He shook his head. "You surprise me, Marcy. The way you do your job, anyone would think you were all for the system."

"I told you. I just work there. I don't make the rules."

"And if you did?"

"I'd try to change things." It seemed a time for sharing, and she told him of her dreams. Children's homes, supported by state and county. They'd have clinics and playgrounds, supervised programs and counselors, well-trained and loving house parents. There would be good care and a securely established routine, the kind of stability that could never be attained when children were shunted from one home to another. She talked eagerly and earnestly about the ideas she had been formulating ever since she'd begun to work with children.

He listened to her and was impressed with her sincerity. More than once he had called her *officious*. But this was a woman who cared. He looked at the blue-green eyes, so alive with love, and with hope for her children. He watched the dimples that disappeared and reappeared in her cheeks, the soft, full mouth. Then, because he couldn't help himself, he kissed her.

She felt the warmth of his encircling arms, the pressure of his mouth against hers. He kissed her again and again, and hot waves of pleasure flowed through her, mounting with the intensity of the incoming tide that beat against the rocks, setting free an erotic yearning deep inside her that clamored to be fulfilled. Her fingers tangled compulsively in his hair and she pressed closer. The sharp cry of a gull echoed her heart's own cry of ecstasy and she wanted him to never let go.

She was unprepared when he gently released her. "I think we'd better check on the children," he said. He was breathing hard, and his voice was hoarse.

He's running away again, she thought in puzzled frustration, as he took her hand and they walked back the way they had come.

CHAPTER TEN

THE RECREATION ROOM was full of children. Some were clustered at big tables, playing dominoes or checkers. In one corner, two games of Ping-Pong were in progress. Other children were gathered in groups, talking and laughing. Ginger detached herself from one group and ran over to them.

"Marcy, I learned a new song!"

"You did? That's great. You'll have to sing it to me when we get to the cottage." But Marcy's eyes were scanning the room. Where was Davey? Steve, too, was searching.

"Davey? Where's Davey?" he asked. "Ginger, where's your brother?"

"Don't know."

Marcy's heart lurched and she felt a tiny ball of fear settling in the pit of her stomach. The fear grew as they toured the building and still didn't find him. Steve approached one of the play leaders.

"He was here a few minutes ago, with that group." She pointed to several boys stationed around a video game, boys a little older than Davey. Marcy thought it was just like Davey to join them—always trying to act older.

When questioned, one of the boys said yes, Davey had been there but he'd gone out.

"That way," he added, indicating the rear door.

When they didn't find him outside, or receive an answer to their calls, Marcy was really frightened. Had he ventured out too far, become lost? Been lured away? She tried to stifle her fears, telling herself she was being ridiculous. He'd probably just returned to the cottage.

"I'll go check the cottages while you look around here," she told Steve. He nodded, already starting toward a wooded area.

She went back into the hall and left Ginger in the care of Amy, a member of the Placer County staff. When she didn't find Davey at either cottage, she ran to meet Steve halfway. He looked just as strained and anxious as she felt.

"I didn't find him, either," she cried. "Oh, Steve what can have happened to him?"

"Nothing's happened to him!" His voice was steady. "He's just playing somewhere. We'll find him. I'll try again behind the rec hall."

Marcy had difficulty keeping up with him. This time they walked farther into the woods, calling his name over and over again. There was no answer, and as it grew darker and colder, her apprehension mounted.

"Shouldn't we give the alarm," she asked, "so other people can help us look for him?"

"Not yet," he said. "Not yet. We'll find him."

"Anybody could get lost in these woods! And suppose he hurt himself and can't move, and—"

"He can hear," Steve said, and he called even louder, "Davey! Davey! Where are you?"

Steve continued to call, but she heard the anxiety in his voice, and an ominous chill swept through her. She remembered his desolation that first day, when the death of his sister had really hit him. Dear God, don't let him lose Davey, too!

"Look, I'm going back to get some of the men," she said, tugging at his sleeve. "They could spread out in different directions and—"

"No!" he said. "I don't want to scare him with a lot of people converging around."

"Scare him! He's lost and he's only five years old, and he's already scared. And you are being impossibly stubborn!" Could it be that he didn't want to face the fact that the boy might be lost, really lost? She felt frustrated, angry and very, very frightened. "You just don't want to ask for help," she shouted. "You don't want people to think you can't take care of your own. And it doesn't matter to you that anything could have happened to him! Don't you realize someone could have lured him away? Some pervert could have wandered up the beach and—"

"The beach!" Steve bolted through the trees toward the beach. Marcy hesitated a moment, looking back toward the conference grounds, then raced after him. Steve was well ahead of her and she scrambled through the dunes, her heart a heavy lump of fear, as the images reeled through her mind. The tide crashing onto the shore . . . Davey, helpless, caught under a rock as the water pounded in, rising higher and higher!

"Davey!" Marcy heard the relief in Steve's voice before she'd even made it as far as the beach. When she got there, she saw the tiny figure some distance away, walking slowly, nonchalantly, in their direction, trailing a stick in the wet sand. Steve was running toward him.

"Davey!" he yelled again. Now there was only anger in the sound, a hot fury that lashed out at the boy. By the time Marcy reached them, Steve was holding Davey by the shoulders and shaking him furiously. Marcy put out a hand to stop him, afraid he would hurt the child. But a moment later, Steve seemed to gain control of himself. Still, he kept a firm hold on Davey and spoke to him sternly.

"Just what are you doing out here alone, young man?"

"I . . . I . . . playing." He looked up at Steve with wide, scared eyes.

"Oh, Davey," Marcy cried, tears of relief running down her cheeks. "We thought you were lost."

"I . . . I wasn't losted." It was to Steve that Davey spoke, his eyes never leaving his uncle's face.

"Didn't I tell you to stay in the recreation hall with the other kids and the teachers?"

Davey nodded, and he looked so frightened that Marcy wanted to cry out, "You said you didn't want to scare him!" But she kept quiet, knowing that this was something between the boy and his uncle, and remembering how terrified Steve had been. When you were that frightened you got angry!

Steve gave Davey's shoulder another little shake. "Now, you listen to me, young man. And you listen hard! When I leave you somewhere, you don't take it upon yourself to walk out. You stay there until I, or the adult I left you with, says you can go. Do you understand that?" Again Davey nodded. "You're responsible to me. Me! You don't take it upon yourself and you don't ask some other kid. You get permission from me. Do you understand?"

"Yes, sir." The same respectful salutation, Marcy noted, that she had heard Davey give his father after a severe reprimand.

"Look at you! You came out here without a jacket, and your feet are all wet! You've been walking in the water?" Steve's voice was still scolding, but more gentle now. He took off his own jacket and wrapped it around Davey. Suddenly he put his arms around the boy and held him close. "I'm sorry I yelled at you, Davey. But I was really scared. I was scared because I care so much about you." He lifted Davey in his arms and hugged him hard, and Marcy saw a glint of tears in Steve's eyes. He cleared his throat, then said, rather gruffly, "We'd better get back to the cottage and put you in a tub of hot water. And I'm not standing for this kind of behavior anymore. Do you understand?"

"Yes," said Davey, his voice muffled against his uncle's neck.

As Marcy walked up the beach beside Steve, who carried Davey, she marveled at the union that had been born between them. It was as if uncle and nephew were enclosed in a world of their own.

"Steve," she heard Davey timidly say.

"Yes?"

"They laughed at me. I didn't want to play with them."

"Oh?" Steve hitched the boy closer to his shoulder. "And that's why you ran away?"

Davey's head bobbed up and down. "They said I was a sissy. Because I was afraid of that cat. It was a big cat, Steve." He raised his head. "A great big black cat, and its eyes...ooh! And it came by me and I was scared and everybody laughed. And I don't like them laughing at me."

Marcy felt a flash of annoyance at those older boys. No wonder they looked so sheepish when they were questioned about Davey.

"Something you'd better get used to," Steve said quietly. "You can't let other people goad you into doing something you shouldn't. Like making you run away. You know what I do when they laugh at me? I just laugh with them."

"You scared of cats?" Davey moved so abruptly that the jacket slipped. Steve, never pausing in his stride, pulled the coat closer around Davey.

"No," he said. "I'm scared of snakes."

"Yes," said Davey, in a voice that indicated that surely everybody was scared of snakes. "Like those big long ones I saw at the zoo that could wrap around you and squeeze you to death?"

"Yeah," Steve said. "There are snakes that are harmless too, but I'm scared of all of them." Marcy noticed that Davey listened intently as Steve told him about his phobia and about how the other men would tease him. He said that just a few months before in Mexico, one of the men had dangled a harmless garden snake in front of him. "He shouldn't have done that. I upset the whole camp. I jumped up, kicking like crazy, threw my grub away and knocked over other food, too. I was like a jumping jack.''

Davey giggled.

"See there?" Steve said. "You're laughing at me, too. Just like they did. But I didn't run away. I just laughed with them and said 'Okay, so I'm scared of snakes. Everybody's scared of something.' ''

Marcy studied Steve's face, still visible through the gathering darkness. His tender concern was evident, and she heard the fatherly conviction in his voice as he told Davey, in his own special way, that it was all right to be afraid, that he need only face up to his fears and never be ashamed. She had not believed it possible. How could she have known that Steve Prescott would be the best thing that could have happened to Diane's children? She reached out and touched him lightly on the arm. He smiled down at her, then set Davey on the ground.

"All right, tiger! You're getting a bit heavy. Hold on to Marcy. She needs help getting through these dunes."

So they walked the rest of the way together, with Davey between them, the three of them holding hands.

It seemed so right.

ACTUALLY, STEVE THOUGHT a few days after he returned home, he hadn't got too much out of those lectures at Asilomar. But, remembering that day on the beach, he was glad he'd gone. He'd been so terrified, he'd lost control, but somehow he had gained Davey's affection. Somehow, that day had brought a change in the boy's attitude.

He liked it. He liked Davey coming home, shouting, "Steve! Steve! Guess what happened at school!" Or, when he'd completed a drawing, "Hey, Steve! Look at this." Or, working with numbers, "Steve, does a three go this way?" Yes, Steve decided, he liked it. Even Ginger, following Davey's lead as usual, had grown a little closer.

Everything seemed to be going well. He'd just about got their legal entanglements straightened out enough to pass on to a lawyer. The real-estate agent had sent pictures of a small, attractive country house in Connecticut. He wanted to show them to Marcy, see what she thought. But he had a feeling that this house was exactly what he'd been looking for. Then, just as everything seemed to be falling into place, two things happened.

First, Mrs. Evans, the almost-suitable housekeeper with excellent references and no encumbrances, tendered her resignation, effective immediately. She had to go back home to care for her bedridden sister whose husband had just died.

"I hate to leave you so suddenly," she said. "But you see how it is, Mr. Prescott."

Yes, Steve told her, he saw how it was, and he gave her a bonus plus a return ticket to New York. Then, inwardly cursing with frustration but resigned to the inevitable, he braced himself to start the housekeeper hunt all over again. He called Mrs. Chisholm who cheerfully agreed to return on an interim basis until he could find another "live-in." She even said she would stay nights when he was out of town, because her sister was now living with her and could look after her children on those occasions.

When he called his secretary in New York and told her to start searching again, he began to understand how things had been with his own father. He'd never had much money at his disposal, and he'd had no one to help him—certainly not an efficient secretary to advertise for applicants and then sift through them. I suppose, Steve thought, feeling more kindly toward his father than he ever had, he did the very best he could.

The day after Mrs. Chisholm's return, Steve got a call from Ginger's nursery school. Ginger had fallen off the monkey bars and hurt her arm. They couldn't tell how seriously because she wouldn't let anyone touch her.

Monkey bars! Steve frowned as he jumped into his car and drove rapidly toward the school. Why would they have such a contraption in a nursery school? And why, since they had one, wasn't it protected underneath with padding or sawdust or something? Anyway, wasn't it too cold and wet for her to play outside?

Poor little kid. So scared she wouldn't let anyone touch her. He had a sudden thought. Maybe she wouldn't let *him* touch her, either. He wondered if he should call Marcy at her office and ask her to come with him.

"Steve!" Ginger cried, running toward him as soon as she saw him. "I hurted myself, Steve!"

"It's going to be all right," he soothed, lifting her gently into his arms, careful to avoid her injury. "We're going to get you all fixed up." He decided to leave his car at the school and take a taxi to the hospital so he could hold Ginger on his lap all the way there. He held and comforted her while the doctor set her arm, which turned out to be broken. And overriding his anger that the school authorities had allowed such a thing to happen, overriding his pity for the tiny child with her arm in a cast, was the exultant thought—*she had run to him.*

"Lord a mercy," Mrs. Chisholm muttered, as she helped a drowsy Ginger out of her jacket. "You've got to be more careful, child. Now, come on and I'll put you to bed. And after you have a nice sleep, I'll make something special for you to eat. I'll even feed you myself." Still fussing tenderly, the housekeeper led Ginger to her room.

SEVERAL DAYS LATER, when the children were playing in Davey's room after dinner, Mrs. Chisholm had a talk with Steve. She poured him a cup of coffee, shaking her head in sympathy. "Lord a mercy, Mr. Prescott, I don't know what you're going to do with these children. You'll run yourself ragged trying to keep up with them. You know what I think? I think you'd better get yourself a wife."

"Ah, Mrs. Chisholm," he said, as he watched her clear the table. "Who'd want a vagabond like me?"

"Humph! Most any woman would like to get her hooks into you, the way you throw your money around!"

"Maybe," Steve said, laughing. "But hooks aren't exactly what I'm looking for."

"Oh, Lord, you're just like everybody else! You want love, sweet love! I'm not talking about love. I'm saying get yourself a wife." She picked up a pile of dishes and started toward the kitchen.

"Hey, wait a minute," Steve called, being in a teasing mood. "Aren't love and marriage supposed to go together like—"

"It just ain't so." Still holding the dishes, she turned to face him. "The way these love matches start today and end tomorrow, you'd be better off hiring yourself a wife!"

"*Hiring* a wife!" Steve had become accustomed to Mrs. Chisholm's outspoken and sometimes outlandish ideas, but this was too much. "Now, Mrs. Chisholm, surely you don't mean—"

"I meant exactly what I said. Hire a wife. You want another cup of coffee?"

"I'll get it," he said, following her into the kitchen. He chuckled as he filled his mug from the steaming pot. "No," he said, shaking his head, "I think it's easier to hire a housekeeper."

"You think so?" Mrs. Chisholm turned from the sink to look at him. "How long have you had these children?"

"Er, I, let's see." He blew on his coffee. "Maybe... almost two months."

"And in those two months you've had three housekeepers, including me twice on a temporary basis. Plus a lot of help from that social worker next door. Isn't that right?"

"Well, yes," Steve admitted.

"The thing is, Mr. Prescott—" she pointed a finger at him "—what you need is more than a housekeeper. You've been hanging around here these past two months and you've hardly been to work at all. You need somebody who can go out and get that child, take her to the hospital and get her arm fixed. And they're growing up. Pretty soon, you'll need somebody to help 'em with their homework. Take 'em to Little League and Girl Scouts. You see, I've been through this. And I can tell you there's more to raising children than keeping a house.''

"You've got a point there," he agreed. He leaned against the counter and took a swallow of coffee. "Now, just in case I find somebody who agrees to shoulder all this responsibility, what do I offer in return?"

"Shoot! Any woman would be glad to settle for the kind of security you could give her." She turned back to the sink and began to load the dishwasher.

"Okay." He smiled. "So I find her, and she agrees. How is all this going to be arranged, this hired marriage business?"

"Just like any other business. You write up a paper. Sign it. What do you call that? A contract? You know more about this kind of thing than I do. You're in business."

"Marriage by contract, huh?"

"Sure. They used to do it all the time. In the olden days, and in lots of those foreign countries. Sometimes they'd contract a marriage even before the child grew up. According to what they could offer each other."

"I see." Steve, still smiling, took another swallow of coffee. "Now suppose something happens—like one of the parties just happens to fall in love with somebody else?"

"But that's just it. You've ruled out the love business, so you're both free to do whatever you please. Fall in and out of love as many times as you want. Just so long as you don't mess up your contract."

Steve choked on his coffee. Mrs. Chisholm paused in her task and looked at him curiously. "You all right, Mr. Prescott?"

Steve cleared his throat, wiped his eyes and handed her the cup. "Yes, I...I'm all right. But you...free love, too!" he exclaimed in mock surprise. "Mrs. Chisholm, you amaze me. I never thought that you...of all people—"

"Oh, go along with you! You're just leading me on. Not paying me a bit of mind. Even though I'm making good sense." She measured out the detergent, locked the dishwasher and turned it on. "You want to marry for love. Love! Probably that young Miss America whose picture you've got sitting on the dresser in there, that lady who keeps calling you all the time. She's pretty, all right, but I doubt she's what you need. I can tell by the way she talks. 'Now how is he managing with the dear little ones?'" she mimicked in tones of exaggerated sweetness and managed to sound, Steve thought, just like Trish. But before he could comment, Mrs. Chisholm gave him a gentle shove. "Now, get away with you. So I can finish in here and bathe those children. And you needn't laugh! You know I'm right."

Still chuckling, Steve went into the living room. Well, she's right about Trish, he decided. Matter of fact, she was right about a lot of things.

"I'm going now. See you in the morning," Mrs. Chisholm said an hour or so later, as she bustled toward the door. "You think about what I told you, Mr. P."

"I'm thinking, I'm thinking!" Steve protested laughingly, as he opened the promised bedtime storybook. The children, already in their pajamas, were waiting, Davey on the arm of his chair, and Ginger on his lap. She'd snuggled as close as she could get, considering that she had a cast on one arm and a tight hold on Lilli Ann with the other.

"Oh, come on in, Miss Wilson," he heard Mrs. Chisholm say. "I'm just leaving."

Then the door shut, and Marcy was standing there in jeans and a pullover. She held a basket in her hand, and she looked, Steve thought, absolutely bewitching. How did she manage to look that way no matter what she wore? The things Mrs. Chisholm had said spun crazily in his mind. Marcy! If he were going to hire a wife . . . But—he couldn't do a crazy thing like that!

Marcy's breath caught in her throat as she observed the little group by the fire. They looked so . . . so right. Her heart warmed at the thought that this man had so quickly gained the trust and affection of these children. She wished . . . What did she wish?

"What's that, Marcy? What you got?" Ginger scrambled down from her uncle's arms and Marcy suddenly noticed the cast.

"Ginger! What happened?"

"I fell and I broke it. And look, the doctor signed the cast. Will you sign it too, Marcy?"

"Oh, baby, of course I will. But you must be more careful." Marcy put down the basket and started toward Ginger. But Ginger was distracted by the mewing sound coming from the basket and ran to see.

"Marcy, you've got a kitten! Where did you get him? Can I hold him?" She ran back to deposit Lilli Ann in Steve's lap and went to kneel by the basket. "Let me hold him."

"Sit down first." Marcy placed the kitten in Ginger's lap. "Now you have to be gentle." As Ginger stroked the kitten, Marcy glanced at Davey. Making a routine call at one of her foster homes earlier that day, she'd been offered her choice from a litter of kittens. She had immediately thought of Davey. Maybe, if he began with such a tiny kitten, he could overcome his fear of cats. He did seem curious, but so far had not moved from the safety of his uncle's chair. Finally it was Steve who persuaded him to approach the kitten.

"Come on. Maybe we men had better take a look at what Marcy dragged in." The four of them sat on the floor and watched the kitten vainly trying to catch the rubber mouse Ginger dangled before him.

"No, Ginger!" Davey cried. "You're teasing him. Here, kitty. I'll get it for you."

Marcy held her breath as Davey took the mouse from Ginger and gave it to the kitten. Then, cautiously reaching out one finger, he stroked the soft gray ball of fur. Marcy felt Steve's touch on her arm and looked across to see him wink at her.

"That was a very thoughtful, very smart thing you did," he told her much later, when the children were in bed.

"I think so too," she said with a grin. "And just as soon as Davey becomes more accustomed to Mr. Kitty Cat, I'm giving him to you, litter box and all."

"Thanks a lot." Steve grimaced. "Hey, wait a minute," he said, as she started to pick up the basket. "I want to show you something." He took an envelope from the coffee table and sat down on the floor beside her, spreading out the pictures. "This is a place in Connecticut that I might be buying. What do you think?"

"Oh, Steve, it's beautiful! Look at all these trees for Davey to climb."

"And there's a small stable. See? Right here. They can have their ponies."

"It seems perfect, Steve."

He showed her the pictures and talked about the house. Six bedrooms with servant quarters, on six acres of ground. How large a staff did she think he would need to care for the place? He was going up next week to look at it and check on schools. Did she like it? Did she think it was a good plan?

"Perfect! Beautiful!" she said over and over again, through the constriction in her throat. She had to blink rapidly to hold back the tears. She smiled and talked brightly about what a lovely house it was, what a great setting. But never in her life had she felt such a wave of sadness and longing. She couldn't bear to think of this apartment empty and the children so far away. And Steve. She watched him as he talked, watched that sweet smile, the

way his eyes crinkled. Steve. Oh, God! It was Steve she
would miss. She...she...dear Lord, she loved him! The
realization was such a shock to her that she missed his next
words.

"What...what did you say?" she stuttered.

"I said would you like to live here?" he asked, his finger
on the picture of the house.

"Oh, why, yes. Of course. Almost anybody would like to
live in a place like this."

"No. What I mean is, er..." He hesitated. "Er, hey,
Marcy, would you marry me?" He was astounded. Had he
meant to say that? Still, it seemed right. Mrs. Chisholm...

"Would I...?" She stared at him, hardly believing that
he had said it. But he had. The joy welled up in her, filling
her heart with so much gladness that—

"Now, wait a minute," She was looking so shocked that
he felt he had to explain quickly. "I don't mean a real marriage. It would be more like...like a job."

"A job?" But hadn't he said *marry*?

"I know it sounds crazy. But it does make sense. Actually, Mrs. Chisholm suggested it."

Marcy listened to him explain something she couldn't
understand, something Mrs. Chisholm had said about how
he needed more than just a housekeeper, and what he should
do was hire a wife. *Hire a wife?* His words seeped through
the confusion of her muddled thoughts. She was astounded
that anyone would think of such a thing! How dare he suggest that she... She had thought... No! She stifled the
feeling, refusing to acknowledge the hurt and the disappointment.

"Marcy, I vowed a long time ago that I would never fall
in love with anyone. I don't want...I don't believe in love,
in this love-forever-after stuff." His own mother. He had
loved her so much! And she had just walked away. Had
never come back. "What Mrs. Chisholm said makes sense.
It makes good sense. We'd both be free. Emotionally free,

I mean. We could go our separate ways. You wouldn't have to answer to me for anything. If there was someone else in your life I'd . . . well, I'd just look the other way.''

"Oh. I see. Open marriage, you mean?'' She was surprised to find that she could speak so calmly.

"Well, yes. Of course, we'd both have to be discreet. But you could have, er, friends, and so could I.''

"I see.'' *You could have as many women as you chose, couldn't you? You just wouldn't have to be sneaky about it.* She felt a rising tide of anger.

"But we'd both always be there,'' he said. "For the children.''

"I see. For the children.''

"Legally, you'd really be my wife, Marcy. You could have anything you wanted. Share everything I own.''

"I see.'' *Everything but love.*

"What do you think, Marcy?''

"I think,'' she said, making her voice sound pleasant, "that Mrs. Chisholm, whom I would never have suspected of such modern ideas, has come up with an excellent plan. And I think it's marvelous of you. Such a grand gesture. Really wonderful to make such a tremendous sacrifice for Davey and Ginger. To contract a marriage for the sake of those children. And I am sure—'' her voice trembled as she stood up "—I am sure that somewhere among your acquaintances, you will find a perfect woman, someone who will be glad to contract such a marriage. But it will not be me!''

"Oh, but Marcy,'' Steve cried, getting to his feet and gazing seriously down at her, "there's nobody else, no other woman who could love the children as much as you do. Wait,'' he said, as she picked up her basket. "Listen, I—''

"I've heard enough! And you listen, Steve Prescott. I'm sorry, but I'm not as modern as your Mrs. Chisholm. And I'm not as self-sacrificing as you. And I do believe in that love-forever-after stuff. And I will not enter into any business marriage.''

''Oh, now, Marcy, don't feel like that. It wouldn't be . . . Look, you and I . . . we get on well together.''

She stared at him, suddenly remembering the way he had kissed her, the way she had felt. Here was a man who didn't believe in love but was an expert in the physical expression of it. She was so distressed by the thought, so ashamed of the erotic sensations aroused by it, that she grabbed at the basket, frightening the kitten, who jumped out. She scrambled after him, dumped him back in his basket and ran out, slamming the door behind her, rushing to the safety of her own apartment, hurrying, before the tears came.

CHAPTER ELEVEN

SHE COULDN'T CRY! She wasn't crying. She had no reason to cry!

Safe at last in the seclusion of her own apartment, Marcy brushed a tear from her cheek and placed the basket near the fireplace. She sank onto her knees beside it, picked up the kitten and held him close. She stroked him, trying to sort out the tangled web of her emotions.

"You're a darling little kitty cat. You're going to love living here with me," she crooned, trying to deny the hurt and disappointment that were sweeping through her. The shame!

No. Not shame!

Yes. Shame! All he had to do was hold out his arms, and you would have fallen into them before he could say "I love you"—which, please note, he did not say!

No. That's not true. I would not have fallen into his arms. And I was not waiting for protestations of love! Marcy bit her lip and shook her head vehemently.

"I can't keep calling you 'Kitty.' What am I going to call you?" Her finger traced his delicate backbone, and the kitten purred with emphatic contentment.

She'd planned to ask Davey to name him. Davey. Ginger.

Marcy Wilson, you'd better keep away from those kids. They'll be gone soon. And Steve. Steve will be gone.

You're in love with him!

No. It just wasn't possible. She couldn't be in love with a man who was insensitive enough to...*hire a wife*! He was impossible! He was an idiot! What made him think she would consent to such a ridiculous arrangement? Did he imagine she was so eager to get married that she'd jump at some unconventional half-baked idea like that!

Oh! She was still furious. She felt feverish and restless. She wanted to get outside, in the fresh brisk air, and run and run and run through the park. But she couldn't, it was too late and too dark. Quickly she flung open her patio door, then tugged the minitrampoline out of the hall closet.

The little kitten purred, stretched, placed one paw over the other and watched with interest as his new mistress bounced and bounced and bounced, all the while muttering to herself, "He's crazy. Absolutely crazy! Impossible! How dare he suggest such a thing!"

WELL, DAMN IT! He had fumbled that one. Steve gave a log a vicious kick, and slammed the fire screen shut.

Maybe he'd taken the wrong approach. No, damn it! She hadn't listened.

It made sense. The more he thought about it, the more sense it made. For her, too. Here she was, working so hard at such an impossible job, frustrated because she couldn't find the perfect home for every problem child. And what did she get for all that work? Peanuts! Otherwise her bank account wouldn't be overdrawn and she wouldn't have to struggle through her bills with that Peter-Paul routine. They obviously weren't paying her enough to live on.

If she married him, she'd never have to skimp. For a moment he mused on that thought, anticipating the pleasure—to take care of her, to give her anything she wanted.

Well, damn it! What did she want? He ran a distracted hand through his hair as he paced the floor.

Love. She wanted *love*. The very word frightened him. Never, not even in the deepest throes of sensual passion, had he whispered the words "I love you" to any woman. Love meant commitment. Promise. And promise of pain when it was over. Mrs. Chisholm had the right idea. If you ruled out love, you ruled out pain. Love was a game people played, making promises of "forever," promises they never intended to keep.

Suddenly he stopped pacing, and stood very still.

Was someone making such promises to Marcy? That Gerald guy? Good old-fashioned friendship, she'd said. Horn Rims? What had she said about Horn Rims? Either one of them could be telling her *anything*! Marcy was so gullible. And she'd said it herself—she believed in that love-forever-after stuff. If a guy played the "I love you" game and played it long enough...

But if she married him, she'd have everything to gain and nothing to lose. He wasn't playing games. He'd been honest with her. Didn't she know she'd be better off with him than falling for the love game? Didn't she know that? He reached for his phone. He'd call her and tell her, right this minute. Then, through the wall, he heard it—that rhythmic jumping. Did she get on that blasted trampoline every time she got mad?

He took his hand from the phone. Not tonight. Give her time to cool off. She'd run out of here fighting mad. And just because he'd asked her to marry him!

Tomorrow. He'd take her out to dinner. He'd convince her that it made sense. That it was to their mutual benefit. And to the children's. One thing he was sure of. If he did hire a wife, arrange a contract marriage, whatever, it wouldn't be with anyone but Marcy Wilson!

HE PHONED before she went to work the next morning. "Marcy, we need to talk."

"I don't think so." Cold. Crisp.

Damn it! She was still mad. "Look, you haven't heard me out."

"I've heard all I need to hear. And I'm in a hurry. I don't want to be late for work."

"Wait. Wait. Don't hang up. Listen, how about dinner tonight?"

"I'm busy tonight."

He might have known. "Lunch? How about lunch?"

"I don't think I can make it. I'm really busy today."

"Oh, for Pete's sake! They do let you eat, don't they? I'll meet you at your office. See you then." He hung up quickly before she could protest.

Busy! He looked out the patio door at the pouring rain. He just bet she'd be busy. Probably sitting at her desk doing paperwork. Nobody with any sense would be out in this weather. The wind whistled around the building and the rain was coming down in sheets.

He got to her office about eleven, and it was a good thing he did, for she was on her way out. In this weather? He couldn't believe it. But there she was. Black umbrella bent against the wind, black raincoat whipping around her legs. Black ankle boots plodding through the puddles to her car. Trust Marcy to be all matched up, he thought, as he turned up the collar of his raincoat and hurried after her.

"Wait! I thought we were going to lunch."

"I told you I don't have time to go to lunch. I've got to go out and transfer this kid to another home."

"Then let me take you. We could stop for a bite on the way and—"

"No, thanks. I prefer to drive myself." She was having a struggle trying to hold on to the umbrella while she unlocked the car. He took the umbrella from her and held it while she got in, protesting that he could take her wherever she needed to go. When she shook her head and reached for the umbrella, he went around to the other side of the car and slid in beside her.

"You should always lock both doors," he said, grinning. "Anybody could get into your car."

"I can see that," she snapped.

"I'd rather drive, but if this is the way you want it, I won't complain," he said as he placed the umbrella on the floor behind his seat.

"This isn't the way I want it," she said through clenched teeth. "Why don't you get out and let me go about my business!"

"Who's stopping you? Drive on. We can have our little discussion en route."

"If it's the same little discussion you started last night, there's no point. Look, I'm already late."

"So drive on." He pushed the seat back to make more room for his legs.

"Oh!" She put the car in gear and swung out of the parking lot with such a terrific burst of speed that he was jerked forward.

"Be careful!" he shouted. "Safety first and all that—"

"Fasten your seat belt if you're scared." She drove onto the freeway, never slackening her speed.

"It's all right. Quite all right." He relaxed against the seat. "I'm perfectly willing to risk life and limb just to have a little straight talk, knowing that should I expire in the attempt, Ginger and Davey will be safe in the arms of Placer County Child Welfare."

"Oh, be quiet!" she said. But their speed diminished a trifle and he couldn't help smiling. Even so, the little Volkswagen rocked dangerously, buffeted by wind and rain.

" 'Over hill, over dale! Through the wind and the hail, And those caissons go rolling along,' " he sang.

"Oh, be quiet," she said again.

"All right, all right," he said serenely. "But, if you ask me, this is a hell of a day to transfer a child."

"Life's little tragedies don't stop for the weather," she informed him crisply. "And it's hard enough for a child to be moved from one house to another, without being delayed from one day to another."

Suddenly he felt depressed. Sorry for any child who had to be shoved around like that. She had pulled off the highway now, pulled up before a neat little bungalow.

"Can I help?" he asked.

"Yes," she said, reaching behind him for the umbrella. "Get in the back seat. Angie will have to sit up front so I can talk to her."

The back seat was a tight squeeze, and he was made even more uncomfortable when Marcy returned and pushed a suitcase in beside him. Angie was a pale-faced little girl of about eight with wide frightened eyes. She was crying softly. Marcy did not start the car immediately, but sat for a time talking quietly with the little girl.

From the conversation, Steve gathered that the child had been abused by her mother, had been taken to an emergency home and was now being transferred to a more permanent foster home.

"Your mother's going through a very hard time right now," Marcy told her. "She wants you to stay with Mrs. Enright for a while, until things get better. You'll like Mrs. Enright. She's very nice, and she has cows and chickens. And she has another little girl just about your age.... Of course you'll see your mother. She'll come and visit you very soon."

Marcy finally started the car, but she kept talking, reassuring the child as she drove. By the time they reached the farmhouse, Steve felt like crying himself. How did Marcy stand it? Sad cases like this, day after day after day.

When Marcy and Angie went into the house, he climbed out of the car and stood for a moment in the steady downpour, stretching his legs. Then he got back in. The rain beat on the roof and washed against the windshield. He stared through the rain at the split-rail fence, thinking about the little girl, wondering about her future. He hoped she would be happy.

"Doesn't it ever get you down?" he asked Marcy when she finally returned. "This kind of situation over and over again?"

"Somebody has to do it."

He was silent as she drove out of the farmyard and back onto the freeway. It was some time before he could force his mind to return to his own predicament. He wanted to take a more diplomatic approach this time. Last night, lying awake, he'd rehearsed it several times. But now, everything he'd planned to say was completely gone from his mind.

"I'm going back east next week," he ventured. "To look at that place. Maybe make an offer."

"That's nice."

"I thought you might take a few days off and go with me. To help me decide."

She gave him a quick incredulous glance. "Fly to New York? You must be nuts. I think you're perfectly capable of making a decision all by yourself."

"Marcy, listen to me." He paused. Hell, what *had* he planned to say? Whatever it was, he'd meant to say it in some quiet, exotic restaurant. Not racking about in this little car in the middle of a windstorm, having to shout above the roar of traffic, the clatter of those damned windshield wipers. "Look, you haven't had lunch. Couldn't we stop somewhere and—"

"No, I don't have time," she was saying when the car suddenly swerved and began to bump along, crazily out of balance. She managed to pull to the shoulder and stop. "Darn," she said. "I think I have a flat tire."

"Darn!" he said ten minutes later, as he placed the last lug in the hubcap, then wrenched the wheel free. "No wonder it went flat. You were riding on threads, Marcy. Will you stop hovering over me with that umbrella!"

"I just want to help."

"You can help by staying out of my way," he said, lifting the wheel toward the trunk.

She followed, still trying to shield him with the umbrella. "This is awful," she moaned. "I knew I should have bought tires last month."

"It appears that you should have," he said, as he loosened the spare from its rack. "This one doesn't look much better than the one that blew. Marcy, will you please get in the car? There's no need for both of us to get soaked."

"But I want to help. What can I . . . can I hold something?"

He put down the tire, took her none too gently by the arm and herded her into the passenger seat.

"Get in," he ordered, taking the umbrella and closing it. "And take this thing with you." He handed it to her, then slammed the door. Wiping the rain from his face, he returned to his task.

"Women! 'I knew I should have bought tires last month,'" he repeated to himself. "From the looks of these she should have bought them last year. And the way she drives..." He cursed as he shoved the wheel into place. She could have been killed, driving on tires like these. As he tightened the lug nuts, he shuddered and it was not from the cold.

"I'm sorry," she said, when he at last slid into the driver's seat. "I knew we should have called Triple-A. You're wet through."

"You're right about that. Just as wet as I would have got if I'd walked to a telephone." He surveyed the traffic, then pulled onto the freeway. "I don't understand you, Marcy. I really don't. Driving on tires like these. It's downright dangerous. Don't you know that?"

"Yes. I know." She bit her lip. "I meant to get tires. But . . . well, something came up."

I just bet it did, he thought. Robbing Peter to pay Paul, and never mind about essentials like tires! That settled it. She'd better marry him. She needed taking care of.

"Where are you going?" she asked, as they turned off the freeway.

"To the nearest garage. We're not driving another mile on those threads."

"Oh, for goodness' sake," she protested. "That spare will certainly last until we get back to the office. I'll take care of it tomorrow."

"Yeah." I just bet you will!

"Really, Steve, you needn't bother."

"I'm bothering. You could kill yourself driving on these bald tires."

"My tires are none of your business, Steve Prescott."

"Now you tell me!" he said, grinning. "If you'd told me that half an hour ago, I wouldn't be all wet and half-frozen."

"Oh, you know what I mean! I...listen, I'd rather go to Pete's gas station in Auburn. I trust him." Pete, Marcy was thinking, would let her charge a tire until she got paid. But Steve had already pulled into a gas station and was getting out of the car.

"You have tires to fit a Volkswagen?" he asked the attendant.

"Sure," the man answered. Marcy's heart sank. Her Visa was up to its limit. But maybe she had enough in her bank account for one tire. How much did the darn things cost?

"We'll take five," Steve said.

Five! She jumped out of the car and ran around to confront them. "No, Steve, we don't need five. We—" Steve's lips were on her parted mouth before she could finish the sentence. Afterward, she was too stunned to speak.

"We certainly do need five, honey," Steve said, shaking her gently. "*You* didn't have to get out in the rain to change a tire. Wives!" he exclaimed, turning to the attendant. "They think all a car needs is gas." He took his wallet from his pocket and handed the man a credit card. "You'd better fill it up and check the oil. Take all the time you need.

We'll be in the coffee shop across the street. Come on, sweetheart." Steve put an arm around Marcy and propelled her out of the station.

"Steve Prescott!" she said, panting as he hurried her across the street before the light changed. "I didn't want all those tires. And you told that man . . . You made him think I'm your wife!"

"Only way to shut you up," he said, reaching for the door of the coffee shop.

"You had no right to give anyone the impression that we're—"

"Sssh!" he whispered. "Folks will think we're having a spat."

"That's just what we are having!" she snapped. But he only smiled.

"Two," he said to the hostess. "Just my wife and myself."

A joke! Love, marriage—it was all a big joke to him. She followed the hostess across the restaurant, bright with Christmas lights and decorations. Only a few tables were occupied, since the noon-hour rush was over.

"Coffee. Hot, hot coffee," Steve said to the waitress, as soon as they were settled in one of the more secluded booths. "Coffee, Marcy?"

She nodded, her anger fading as she looked at him. His hair was still damp and his clothes were soaked, because he'd taken off his raincoat to change the tire. He must have been chilled to the bone. And he had not once complained. Suddenly, she was glad for his sake that they'd stopped. Glad they could rest for a while in the warmth of this place filled with the rich aroma of coffee and the soft, haunting sound of Christmas music. She had to admit that she was grateful to Steve. What would she have done if he hadn't been with her?

"I . . . I do appreciate your changing the tire," she said, "and everything." Oh, Lord! How was she ever going to repay him? Maybe she could borrow the money from Jennifer. "And I'll pay you for the tires as soon as I can," she added.

He waved his hand in a gesture of dismissal.

"Consider it a gift—for both of us."

"Both of us?"

"Your life and my sanity." He chuckled. "I'd have nightmares thinking of you skidding around on those tires."

"All the same," she started to say, then silently finished, *I am going to repay you,* as the waitress placed two mugs of steaming coffee before them and asked if they were ready to order.

"Steak sandwich for me," Steve said. "Marcy?"

She scanned the menu quickly. "Split pea soup," she decided.

"And soup for my wife," he said, his lips twitching.

"You should stop that!" Marcy scolded when the waitress had left.

"Stop what?"

"Joking about this wife business."

"Who's joking?" He was still grinning as he spoke, but then, looking almost serious, he reached across the table to take her hand. "Think about it, Marcy. Really think about it. It would be a good deal."

"A good deal?" she repeated, drawing her hand away. That was how he thought of marriage. A good deal!

"Sure." He took a swallow of coffee, then put the mug down. "All right. Admittedly it's a good deal for me. I'd never worry about Ginger and Davey if you were there to look after them. But it would be a great plan for you, too, Marcy. Don't you see that?"

"No. I don't think so. And really, Steve, I don't want to discuss it."

"There would be a lot of advantages for you," he continued as if she hadn't spoken. "It's funny, you know. I got the impression you were so efficient. And I guess you are—

with your job and the children. But not with yourself." He shook his head. "You need somebody to take care of you, Marcy."

"I've been taking pretty good care of myself for some time!"

"That's debatable, Marcy. Anyway, I'm offering you a very practical plan."

Practical!

"I don't want to talk about it!" she snapped. "Just because you changed my tire doesn't mean you've changed my mind."

"But that's just it. You need somebody around to change your tires. To look after things like that." *Pay your bills.* He leaned toward her. "I'm not trying to shackle you or tie you down. You'd be perfectly free. And listen, I thought of something else. All that stuff you were telling me about the kind of children's home you would like to see developed? You said it could be a better alternative than the foster parent program."

"Yes." Strange he should remember that.

"Well, if you married me, you wouldn't be working in the system. And you wouldn't be under any obligation to them. You could take your time. Write up your ideas, plan the kind of program you prefer. And then make a proposal or whatever you call it. Maybe some county or foundation could be talked into starting that kind of home on an experimental basis. My company would contribute to the funding. I promise. You might accomplish more with the stroke of a pen than you could ever accomplish running around with these kids the way you do. Can't you see that, Marcy? Later on, other counties might decide to copy the idea."

"You know something, Steve? You have a point there. I wonder why I never thought of it myself. But," she added, shaking her head, "I don't have to marry anyone to write up a plan."

"But don't you see? If you're going to come up with an effective proposal, you'll have to be independent. Free to speak your own piece. Under no obligation to anyone, including me. Except for the kids, of course. We'd both be free to pursue our own interests. Wouldn't you like that?" He paused, as the waitress brought their orders. "Very quick service. Thank you." He smiled up at the waitress, and Marcy felt a stab of pain as she watched the girl glow under the influence of that smile.

Yes, she thought. He'd be free to smile, to touch or kiss anyone he wanted . . . Tricia? And I would go crazy with jealousy. No. I wouldn't be jealous. I couldn't be. I'm not in love with him!

"Marcy, are you in love?"

"What?" His question caught her by surprise, and she felt her face grow warm.

"Are you in love with someone?"

"No. No, indeed I'm not," she answered, perhaps a shade too emphatically.

"Then why not marry me?" he asked. "It might save you from heartbreak. Believe me, Marcy," he said earnestly. "This love stuff never lasts. It only leads to pain."

CHAPTER TWELVE

MARCY MANAGED TO RESIST all his arguments. She was relieved when they finally picked up her car and drove back to Auburn, where he reluctantly left her at her office. His voice with its joking, cajoling persuasions still lingered in her ears. His face swam before her, obscuring the forms on her desk, so that she accomplished very little in the late afternoon. She would have to stay away from him, would have to keep busy with other people, other things.

"I think I'll spend this weekend with you at the cabin," she told Jo. "I'd like to do some skiing."

"Oh, so nice of you to let us have you over." Jo laughed. "Are you driving up with us tonight?"

"No, I can't," Marcy said, remembering her date with Tom. "I'll probably get Tom or Gerald to drive me up in the morning. Then I'll stay over and come back with you guys Sunday night. Okay?"

"Okay," said Jo. "See you tomorrow."

At home, Marcy fed the kitten by herself, not calling Davey as she'd originally intended.

She must detach herself. She was too involved with these two children who would soon be out of her life altogether.

"Guess you'll have to be my company, Mr. Kitty Cat." She rubbed her chin against his soft fur and tried not to feel so disheartened. Still holding the kitten, she picked up the phone and called Jennifer. Jennifer, too, sounded a little depressed, but said she'd be glad to lend Marcy the money to pay for the tires. She said she was relieved Marcy had got her old ones replaced; bad tires were dangerous in this weather.

Marcy then washed her hair, and stood a long time in the shower, letting the hot steamy water pour over her. I'm pretty lucky, she thought as she toweled herself dry, to have the kind of hair that doesn't have to be set. In fact, I'm not too bad at all, she decided, brushing her hair and letting it fall into the full natural waves that framed her face.

I'm a chic size eight, and I'm smart. Well...maybe not too smart. I go overboard buying nice things, and I do lose track of my money sometimes. So I couldn't say I'm *smart* smart. But I'm not lazy, either. I do my job and I do it well. I'm good-natured and good company. And I can ski and swim and play a pretty fair game of tennis.

I'm *me*. I'm more than a housekeeper and a nanny, Steve Prescott!

She paused, her mind lingering on the name. She was seeing that dark hair, tumbled and wet, one lock falling across his forehead. Seeing his smile, remembering the feel of his arms around her, the touch of his lips on hers. Suddenly, her thoughts went racing wildly in another direction, the very direction she'd been trying to avoid.

I could love you, Steve Prescott! I could make you happy.

Tom took her dancing, and Marcy was glad she'd worn her turquoise silk with the full skirt that swirled so gracefully around her legs. Tom was a good dancer, and they both enjoyed the evening, staying out until two in the morning. Even so, he said he'd be happy to drive her up to Jo's the next morning.

STEVE HAD HEARD MARCY come in from work. Later, he heard the knock on her door, heard her go out with... He wasn't sure. He thought it was Horn Rims. He never paused in his reading of *A Visit From St. Nicholas*.

She'd told him she had a date. That was okay. "We'd each be free to go our separate ways," he had said. And he meant it. No ties. No commitments. He hoped she realized how he was taking it all in stride, all her men friends and her dates. He shifted Ginger in his lap and read on. "'The moon, on the crest of the new-fallen snow...'"

Of course she'd have to schedule time for the children. She was out tonight. Okay. Maybe in the morning, they could, all four of them, go down to the Nut Tree for brunch. "'And then in a twinkling I heard on the roof the prancing and pawing of each little hoof.'"

He wondered whom she was with. Probably Horn Rims. He hoped she had a miserable time.

MARCY REALLY HADN'T BELIEVED Tom when he told her to be ready at five. But there he was. And he didn't object when she explained that they had to take Mr. Kitty Cat with them.

"Mr. Kitty Cat?" he asked. "Doesn't he have a real name?"

"I'm still trying to decide," Marcy said, thinking of Davey and wondering if the poor little kitten would be forever nameless. Because part of her was waiting for Davey to name him, and part of her was keeping as far away from Davey as she could.

She liked Tom, she decided, although he did keep harping on the necessity of accumulating a stock portfolio. She didn't bother to tell him that she couldn't afford even *one* stock. Still, it was nice of him to drive her up to Jo's place. He stayed for most of the day and went skiing with her. Then she and Jo made spaghetti. The boys were ecstatic over Mr. Kitty Cat.

On Sunday, Marcy took Jo's boys to the beginners' hill, so Jo and her husband could go skiing together on the higher slopes. They drove back very late Sunday night.

There! That took care of the weekend.

WELL, DAMN! She'd been away the whole weekend.

When he found she wasn't there Saturday morning, he and the children had gone to the Nut Tree anyway. The kids seemed to enjoy the brunch and the rides. But...something was missing.

Marcy. He missed her laugh, seeing her dimples appear and disappear, watching her play with the kids.

She wasn't there Sunday, either, and he wondered where she was spending the weekend. And with whom.

MONDAY, SHE GOT UP EARLY and had breakfast at a coffee shop near the office. Her phone was ringing when she got to work. Her heart sank when she heard Mrs. Emory's voice.

"Somebody's got to talk to that boy, Miss Wilson. He's really getting out of hand."

"Jimmy? Oh, I'm sorry, Mrs. Emory. What's wrong?"

"Well, for one thing, he got in a fight at school last Thursday and got suspended. Had to stay home Friday. I tried to call you, but you weren't there. I just don't know what to do with him, Miss Wilson." The poor woman sounded at her wits' end and Marcy felt guilty that she hadn't been there at such a crucial time.

"Sorry. I was out in the field. I'll try to see Jimmy today. He's a very troubled boy, Mrs. Emory."

"Yes, I know, Miss Wilson. I've been talking to his counselor and he tells me to be patient. I want to help Jimmy, but he seems sassier than ever."

Marcy tried to soothe her, promising to talk with the counselor and with Jimmy. She was glad Mrs. Emory hadn't asked to have the boy removed from her home. At least she was still trying—even if it was as much out of financial need as concern for Jimmy.

Marcy sighed. She did sympathize with the woman, who probably had her hands full with that boy. She decided to visit the school that morning and talk to Jimmy's teacher.

"He's a very bright boy, Miss Wilson. But so belligerent. Always in a spat with some kid or other."

Marcy picked Jimmy up after school and the first thing he asked her was, "Can't I go back and live with my mom, Miss Wilson?"

"Not yet, Jimmy. You know your mother isn't well." How could she tell him that she didn't even know where his mother was?

"I don't want to stay with Mrs. Emory. They don't like me."

"Oh, Jimmy, of course they do."

"No, they don't. Nobody likes me."

"I like you. And your teacher likes you. She tells me you're very bright. And you're on the soccer team. Do you like playing soccer?"

The boy's eyes brightened. "Yes, and I'm good, Miss Wilson. Coach made me the goalie, and Sid Bates got mad. He thinks he's the best, and he ought to be the goalie."

"Sid. Is that the boy you had the fight with?"

"Yes." Jimmy looked down at his scuffed shoes, then he looked at her. "But he started it. He said I couldn't be the goalie 'cause I didn't have no soccer shoes."

Somehow, in a roundabout way, Marcy learned that soccer shoes were the immediate problem. Jimmy was the only boy on the team without them. "Mr. Emory said there was no money to buy soccer shoes." But Jimmy had run errands for the man next door, and when the man gave him five dollars he went to buy the shoes himself. Here Jimmy's eyes opened wide.

"Do you know how much soccer shoes cost, Miss Wilson? Sixteen dollars and ninety-five cents. I'm never gonna have sixteen whole dollars."

Marcy had exactly fourteen dollars and some change in her purse.

"For the soccer shoes. You'll have to put your five with it," she told him, as she gave him the money. "All I want you to do is govern your temper. Don't get in any more fights. Smart people don't fight, Jimmy, and your teacher tells me you're very smart.'' She talked with him a long time, encouraging him as much as she could and finally promising to look for another home.

Marcy felt like crying as she drove back to the office. She thought of searching for Jimmy's mother. But, no. If the woman had put her life into some kind of order, made any progress at all, she would have got in touch with them.

Marcy looked over the list of available homes, knowing it would be hard to find the perfect place for Jimmy. A home where he would be cherished and given the attention he craved, the patient discipline he needed. A home where he might be happy. Well, she could ensure that he had adequate food and shelter, but there was nothing she could do to ensure him happiness. She'd just better accept that.

But she could make Ginger and Davey happy. If she married Steve...

Ginger and Davey are happy. Steve will take good care of them. They don't need you.

She remembered Steve's suggestion that she write a proposal for the kind of children's home she envisioned. He'd said some county or foundation might fund it on an experimental basis. She should put her plans on paper, he'd said.

You don't need to marry anybody to do that. You're just making excuses to accept his ridiculous offer—of a marriage that would make you miserable.

Get your mind off yourself, Marcy, and get back to work!

She thumbed through her files. The Stevensons. Jimmy might be happier there. They already had three boys, but they might take another. She'd call them, maybe tomorrow.

After work, she went over to Gerald's and made dinner for the three of them. She played chess with Mr. Sims, and when he'd gone to bed, she listened to records with Gerald until almost midnight. She couldn't keep doing this, she told herself when she finally let herself into her own apartment. She couldn't avoid Steve forever. Well, she'd certainly try to do just that. They had to leave for Connecticut sometime.

Steve phoned her twice the next morning at the office, but she said she was too busy to talk. It was almost noon when she got the call from her sister.

"Marcy, I can't stand it! I can't live without Al."

Without Al? "Jennifer, pull yourself together and tell me what happened."

"He's left me. Oh, Marcy, what am I going to do?"

Marcy had trouble understanding her through the sobs. "Just hang on, Jennifer," she soothed. "I'll be there as soon as I can." She got emergency leave and went straight home to pack. When she drove into the parking lot, she was relieved to see that Steve's car wasn't there.

She scanned the mail and found the promised check from Jennifer. Poor Jennifer. So generous. So unhappy. Marcy decided to deposit Jennifer's check immediately, so she could repay Steve for the tires. She wrote him a check and slipped it into an envelope with a note. Then she packed.

"Oh, what am I going to do with you?" she asked, as Mr. Kitty Cat rubbed against her leg. "I can't handle you and Jennifer, too." And I won't take you next door, she thought. Board him at the vet's? No, he's too young.

Gerald. She picked up the phone.

"Sure," said Gerald. "Swing back by the office and leave your key. I'll get the kitten."

She gave the note for Steve to Mrs. Chisholm. Then she deposited Jennifer's check, left her key with Gerald and drove on to Shingle Springs. She was sorry about Jennifer's plight, but at least it meant she wouldn't be running into Steve during the next several days.

Jennifer's house was in a development designed and controlled by her husband, Al's, company. These were all luxurious custom-built homes, each one located on almost an acre of land. The grounds featured a golf course, several tennis courts, two swimming pools and a very large club-house. The security guard at the entrance phoned Jennifer before waving Marcy on.

Money isn't everything, Marcy thought, as she drove through the well-tended grounds to Jennifer's house.

Jennifer, still in her nightgown and robe, looked awful. She sat at her kitchen table, surrounded by dirty dishes and leftover food, cradling a cup of long-cold coffee in both hands. Her beautiful golden-blond hair was uncombed and lay in tangled disarray around her swollen face. Her eyes were red and puffy. She looked dazed, exhausted, as though she'd cried until there were no more tears. She flung herself into Marcy's arms, and Marcy held her for a long time, soothing her, saying she was not to be upset, that everything was going to be all right. Just as she had said to so many children, Marcy thought.

"Everything is going to be all right. This is Mrs. Blank. You'll be happy here." And then she always held her breath, knowing that everything was not going to be all right. But hoping the child would be happy anyway.

STEVE STOOD in his living room, drumming his fingers on the mantel, holding the note Mrs. Chisholm had given him.

> I can never thank you enough for the roadside service in the rain. But I can repay you for the tires. Thank you again.

So! She was avoiding him. That was plain.

Well, Miss Marcy Wilson, you can run, but you can't hide forever. I'll see you tonight, he thought, tearing the check and tossing it into the fireplace.

He waited for her to come home. When he heard footsteps moving toward her apartment, he quickly stepped out to confront her. It was Gerald, and he was opening Marcy's door. *Apparently with his own key.* Steve managed a nonchalant nod, then walked right past him and kept going all the way to the parking lot, where he jumped into his car and roared off.

Damned if he'd ask that smug-faced guy where Marcy was! And what the hell was he doing with a key to her apartment?

"I DIDN'T THINK Al would ever leave me. I couldn't believe it," Jennifer said.

Marcy couldn't believe it, either. Those two had seemed so happy, so much in love when they got married.

This love stuff never lasts! That was what Steve Prescott had said. Marcy shook her head, impatient to rid herself of the memory. When she turned to Jennifer again, her voice was sharper than she'd intended.

"You mean he just walked out? For no reason?"

"Well…not exactly. He was late coming home last night and I really lit into him. And he said he was sick and tired of me being suspicious all the time for no reason. Then he grabbed some clothes and walked out."

"Now that just sounds like a temporary rift to me. Come on. Help me unpack and you can tell me all about it. Where do you want me to stay?"

"Stay with me. I can't stand to be by myself. And it's not a temporary rift, Marcy. It's been coming a long time. I knew it was going to happen." She took Marcy's hand as they walked slowly from the kitchen to the bedroom.

Surprisingly, the rest of the house was in perfect order. Plants, sofa pillows, nothing was out of place. Not even an open magazine or an old newspaper thrown carelessly about. The living room looked like a picture in *Better Homes and Gardens*.

The bedroom was another matter. It was a mess. Rumpled bed, discarded clothes tossed everywhere, a pair of Al's dirty socks on the floor. While Marcy unpacked, Jennifer fell across the bed in a miserable heap, and her story poured out in a garbled flood of words.

She'd suspected it all along, she told Marcy. More and more weekends out of town, late nights out when he had to see a client, all those Sundays on the golf course.

"Of course, I always knew. Well, you know, Marcy, how women take to Al. They flatter him and he's so... so...vulnerable."

Marcy picked up her cosmetic case and carried it to the bathroom.

Vulnerable! Gullible was the better word, Marcy thought. Al was well aware of his good looks. He knew that women were attracted to his striking blue eyes and blond hair and he loved every minute of it!

Unlike Steve Prescott, Marcy thought, lingering to straighten and wipe off the cluttered counter. Steve was absolutely unaware of his charms. He just smiled that sweet, lazy, adorable smile, oblivious to its effect. Never guessing how many women were enraptured by the way his eyes lit up and crinkled at the corners.

Marcy went back into the bedroom, and sat on the bed beside Jennifer. "...this divorcée," Jennifer was saying, "who bought a house on the east side of the development this summer. She calls Al at least once a week to come and see about this or that. And when she's not calling him, she's parading around the pool in her bikini. She's got the figure for it, too. But I'm sure that flaming red hair of hers is dyed! Oh, Marcy, I knew from the first that she had her eye on Al!"

Marcy listened to her sister's tearful recital and wondered about Al. It was true that he was easily flattered, but she did not believe him unfaithful.

"Has Al given you any reason to think he's interested in this woman?" she asked carefully.

"Oh, you know Al." Jennifer tossed her head. "He just says it's good business to keep everybody satisfied."

It occurred to Marcy that Al had always worked hard, always spent a lot of time trying to please his customers. But she didn't say anything. She just sat there, holding Jennifer's hand, listening to her tearful saga of suspicions, denials and uneasy reconciliations.

What was happening to her sister's marriage? Marcy wondered. And how had Jennifer become this distraught, unhappy woman? She had always been so cheerful and loving and confident.

"Get up," she said suddenly. "Go take a shower, Jennifer, while I fix us something to eat."

"Oh, Marcy, I'm not hungry."

"Well, I am. And I don't like seeing you looking like something the cat dragged in, when you're one of the prettiest women I know. Now, scoot!"

While Jennifer showered, Marcy made the bed and then went into the kitchen, where she emptied and washed the coffeepot, stacked the dirty dishes in the dishwasher and wiped off the counters and table. She tried to concentrate on Jennifer and Al, but Steve's image kept intruding and she kept hearing his voice making dire predictions about love.

But you're wrong, Steve Prescott, you're wrong! It's *people* who change. They become immersed in their day-by-day existence. Al, too busy making money and pleasing his customers. Jennifer, not busy enough in her picture-book house. It takes a strong love to carry a marriage through the hardships and the monotony of daily living, she thought. And marriage without love hasn't a chance, she told herself fiercely, determined to stamp every vestige of Steve from her mind.

There was little in the refrigerator but a leftover roast that looked as though it should be thrown away. We are definitely going to the grocery store, she decided, heating up a can of soup and setting out cheese and crackers.

Jennifer came into the kitchen, looking considerably better in brown slacks and a beige sweater, and even managed to eat some of the meal Marcy had prepared. Still, she continued to complain about Al. While Jennifer talked, Marcy's practical mind began to sift through the facts. As far as she could determine from what she'd heard, there was no real evidence of "another woman."

"When he took off this morning, it just confirmed what I suspected," Jennifer said, aimlessly toying with her soup-spoon. "I've been watching... waiting for this to happen."

Marcy studied her sister's hurt embittered face. Suspecting... watching... waiting. Was that the key? Had Jennifer driven Al away with her accusations of imagined betrayals? Marcy remembered the Sunday she and the children had spent with a most disagreeable Jennifer.... *If I were Al, I'd spend my Sundays on the golf course too* had been her own reaction. Could it be that Jennifer, even after her marriage, had never stopped competing for Al, had never really believed he loved her, had visualized the day he would leave her?

Visualization. Marcy sat up. Funny how the ideas in that book—ideas she wasn't sure she believed in—kept coming back to her.

Whatever you picture in your mind will come to pass.

"And this morning," Jennifer was saying, "I really confronted him. I told him I wouldn't stand for it anymore. And he said he was sick of my accusations and complaining, and then he walked out. And it isn't just a temporary rift like you think, Marcy. He said he had to go out of town today, but he'd be back to get the rest of his clothes tomorrow evening."

Marcy looked at Jennifer, hardly hearing her. Attitude. How could she change Jennifer's attitude?

"Oh, Marcy, I don't believe he'll ever come back."

"He won't if you keep thinking he won't," Marcy said so sharply that Jennifer gave a start.

"Oh, Marcy, don't say that!"

"Well, you certainly can't mope him back. You've got to change the picture in your mind."

"Picture in my...? Marcy, what are you talking about?"

"I read this book about a technique called visualization. If you want something to happen, you can help bring it about by pretending it's already happened."

Jennifer said the whole thing sounded crazy to her, but Marcy caught her attention with the story about a woman whose husband had asked for a divorce, saying he didn't love her anymore. The woman agreed, only asking him to wait a month. During that month, she put her imagination to work, picturing in her mind the way things had been when her husband loved her. Pretending that he'd never stopped loving her.

"And at the end of the month," Marcy concluded, "it came true. He returned, saying he still loved her and didn't want a divorce after all."

"Marcy, that's not possible."

"It's a true story, Jennifer. It really is possible to change your life by changing your thinking." She had thought it would be difficult to convince her sister, but like a drowning person, Jennifer was grasping at any straw.

"What do I do first?" she asked.

"Start thinking how much Al loves you, how happy you are together."

"But we...he doesn't...he's not even here."

"Thoughts, Jennifer. Thoughts! Take control of your thoughts. In your mind he loves you and you are happy."

"Oh, Marcy. That's not true."

"Listen, darn it! You have to do it with your whole heart and mind. No negatives. Positive thinking all the way. Dwell on how you *want* things to be. Not how they appear on the outside. Say it over and over, out loud if necessary, 'Al loves me. He's coming home.'"

Jennifer regarded her dubiously, but obediently repeated the phrases several times.

"And look happy," Marcy advised. Privately she believed more in action. Al needed to *see* Jennifer being happy. "When did you say Al was coming for his things?" she asked.

"Tomorrow evening."

"Perfect," said Marcy. "Now, the first thing we're going to do is go out and buy a Christmas tree."

"Christmas tree! I can't bear to think of Christmas. And, anyway, it's not even the tenth of the month yet."

"We're starting early. And you love Christmas. Picture this—Al is here with you," Marcy said in her most seductive voice. "The two of you are sitting by the Christmas tree, and he's giving you a diamond bracelet and telling you how much he loves you."

"Oh, Marcy, do you really think . . . ?"

"It's not what *I* think that matters; it's what *you* think. Now put your coat on. We're going out for that tree."

But first Marcy called Tom. Would he come over early tomorrow afternoon, and bring a friend?

"We'll make dinner if you help decorate a Christmas tree. I'm in Shingle Springs with my sister who's going through a bad time and needs cheering up."

When Al did appear the next evening, he seemed dumbfounded to find a jolly group in his living room, decorating a Christmas tree and drinking hot toddies.

"Oh, hello, Al," said Jennifer, who had been carefully coached. "I forgot you were coming. Marcy's here to help me with the tree. This is Phil Glover, and I think you've met Tom Jenkins." Then, as Al nodded to everyone, she added, "Can I get you a toddy or something?"

"Oh, no. No thanks," he said. But Marcy noticed he couldn't take his eyes off Jennifer, who looked absolutely stunning in a green velvet jumpsuit, with her golden hair tousled just right.

"Can you manage with your things?" Jennifer asked sweetly, "Or do you need some help?"

"No. I'll manage."

Marcy couldn't tell whether he was puzzled or disgruntled. Probably both, she thought, winking at Jennifer as he turned away. Her sister bore very little resemblance, now, to the hysterical female he had walked out on just one day before.

STEVE PRESCOTT was frustrated. He hadn't been able to reach Marcy, and all her office would tell him was that she was on emergency leave. He wanted to ask her about the children's Christmas presents. And, yes, he wanted to get her final answer on the Connecticut place.

He just bet that Gerald guy knew where she was, but damned if he'd ask him!

On Thursday, the real-estate agent called and said someone else was dickering for the place he was interested in. If he still wanted it . . .

He took a plane for Connecticut the next day.

CHAPTER THIRTEEN

MARCY WAS PACKING to go home. Al had returned the night before and all was forgiveness, love and happiness in the household.

"Your coming made a big difference," Jennifer told her.

"Nonsense!" Marcy folded her slacks and placed them in the suitcase. "You love each other. You would have patched things up without me."

"Well, yes, I suppose. But, you see, it was our quarreling that drove him away in the first place. And it could have happened again. But it won't, because I'm different now."

"Oh?" Marcy closed her suitcase and looked at her sister.

"I was afraid to be happy, Marcy. Every time Al was out of my sight, I filled my mind with suspicions and... well, negative thoughts." She smiled at Marcy. "You taught me that it was all right to be happy." She had a strange way of putting it, but Marcy knew what she meant.

"Happy thinking," she said, when she kissed her sister goodbye. As she drove away she wondered if happy thinking really did change things. Or just change you inside, so that you were happy even though things on the outside weren't any different at all.

Perhaps it's foolhardy to try to change things into being the way you want them to be, Marcy thought. It's better to think yourself into being happy with the way things are. And that's what I must do, she told herself.

During the time she'd just spent at Shingle Springs, Marcy had been absorbed in Jennifer's problems, so absorbed that she'd been able to stifle her own feelings. But deep inside her, there had been a sense of hopeless desolation. Buried beneath the bravado, beneath the encouraging words uttered for Jennifer's sake, was the hurtful knowledge of her own loss.

She was being ridiculous. How could she lose something she'd never had? *I have to try to make sense of my real world,* she thought. *I must face up to the fact that I am in love with a man who does not love me, who does not want to be committed to anyone.* A man callous enough to try to involve her in a make-believe marriage for his own convenience. How dare he!

How dare you? Are you going to let Steve Prescott muddle up your life?

Definitely not. She'd been happy before she knew him. She would continue to be happy without him.

She sped toward Auburn, full of determination. Of course she wouldn't avoid the children, and she'd be casually pleasant to Steve. But she would certainly be busy, very busy. She would have to catch up on her work, finish her Christmas shopping, mail her Christmas cards.... There would be parties, too. Jo always had a party, and so did her friend, Meg. Yes, she would be busy. And she would be happy if it killed her! She would think happy, and her thoughts would not include Steve Prescott!

"Marcy!" Ginger cried, running out to meet her. "Where have you been, and where is the kitty? You promised we could feed him, and then we couldn't find you."

"I had to go away for a while. The kitty will be home soon, and you can feed him," Marcy said, as she hugged Ginger.

"Steve's gone away," Ginger volunteered. "To...to 'neticut."

"Oh!" Marcy was casual, masking her disappointment. How could she possibly feel disappointed? She didn't want to see Steve; she'd even planned to avoid him. Now she was keenly aware of how much she missed him. How much she longed to see that crooked smile. She had resolved not to be touched by his smile, had braced herself to resist his playful, teasing persuasions—persuasions that were somehow very strong, very sweet. But he wasn't there, and she was not prepared for the emptiness. It felt as though something exciting and vibrant in her life had suddenly been snatched away, leaving a terrible void.

"We're going to 'neticut too," said Ginger. "Pretty soon, we're going. And we're going to have ponies."

"How nice," Marcy said. So he had decided to buy that beautiful home. They would go and live there, and she would stay here. And she couldn't bear it!

Take control of your thoughts, Marcy. Think happy. With life as it is.

"I'm going to buy a Christmas tree," she said. "Will you help me decorate it?" No matter where she planned to spend Christmas, Marcy always had her own tree.

"Oh, yes!" Ginger was delighted. "Can we get it now?"

She bought a small tree, so heavily flocked it seemed weighted down with snow. She and the children decorated it with tiny white lights, golden bells and two white doves. She made an arrangement of frosted magnolia leaves and pine cones for her mantel, and placed a large poinsettia on her dining table. She set a fire blazing in the fireplace. The apartment looked very cheerful and Christmassy. And felt very empty.

She called her mother in Phoenix to ask her plans for the holiday.

"I'm so glad you called," exclaimed her mother, "I've got some wonderful news." She'd just received an airline ticket from Marcy's brother, Bill, along with an invitation to spend Christmas with his family in Japan.

After the call, Marcy sat in her cheerful empty apartment and stared at the fire. The radio was playing a medley of Christmas tunes, and she wondered why the sound of holiday rejoicing made her feel sad. She stood up. Enough of this self-pity! She marched briskly to the phone to call Tom and invite him for dinner the next night. He'd been so nice, helping with Jennifer, and she wanted to return the favor.

Tom said he'd be glad to come, and Marcy went to bed, thinking she might give a Christmas party herself. She thought about her guest list and what she should serve. She thought about Jennifer, happy with Al. She remembered she'd have to get a loan to repay Jennifer for the money she'd borrowed to repay Steve for the tires. That made her smile—she really was robbing Peter to pay Paul. She'd mail the presents for her mother and Bill's family, so her mother would get them before she left for Japan. She tossed and turned and finally fell asleep.

She dreamed she was running, running through the park by the complex. In the middle of the park was a giant flocked Christmas tree, decorated with golden bells and white doves. Steve stood under the tree, smiling, holding out his arms. She ran straight to him, and he gathered her close. She felt warm in his embrace. Then he kissed her, and she heard Christmas music and the bells on the tree began to ring. They clanged louder and louder.

Her bedside phone was ringing. Still half-asleep, Marcy groped for it.

"Hello?" Who on earth could be calling her at this time of night?

"Miss Wilson? Miss Wilson, can you come here?" It was a child's voice, and he was crying.

"Yes, this is Miss Wilson. Who is this? What's wrong?"

"Please, Miss Wilson, would you come and get me?"

"Jimmy?" Marcy sat up in bed. "Is this Jimmy Braxton?"

"Yes, ma'am. Would you come and get me?"

"What's the matter? Let me speak to Mrs. Emory."

"She's not here. I'm—I'm not there. I'm here."

"Where?" Marcy looked at her clock radio. 12:14. "Jimmy, you're not at the Emorys'? Where are you?"

"I don't know exactly. I—"

Marcy, very disturbed now, was about to question him further when a man's voice broke in.

"Hello, ma'am. Pete Turner here. I picked this kid up on the highway."

"On the highway!" Marcy cried. "What on earth—?"

"He was thumbing a ride. But I know damn well no kid this size should be out here this time of night. It's rough out here. All kinds of folk around. He's lucky I picked him up."

"Oh, yes, I'm glad you did. Thank you, Mr. . . ."

"Turner. Pete Turner. I thought I'd better turn him over to the police, but he begged me not to. I . . . well, I hated to get him in trouble. He said you were with the welfare department and you'd take care of it."

"Oh, yes, I will," Marcy said quickly.

"What do you want me to do? I don't want to leave him by himself. It's just not safe."

"No, of course not. Where are you, Mr. Turner?"

"Jake's Place. You know it? A truck stop on Highway 80."

Marcy said she did know it, and that she would come right away. The man promised to wait. She scrambled into a pair of woolen pants and a heavy jacket, her mind in turmoil. What was Jimmy doing out on Highway 80 at this time of night? And if he was missing from the Emorys', why hadn't Mrs. Emory called her? Then she hoped Mrs. Emory hadn't noticed his absence, because Jimmy had run away once before. If he was reported again, and the authorities took him into custody, he might be sent to Juvenile Hall—the last thing he needed. She was convinced he'd do well in the right environment.

But you knew the Emorys weren't right for him. You knew it, Marcy! And you've been so busy with Jennifer, and so busy feeling sorry for yourself, you've hardly given him a thought. Maybe he'd called when she was on leave and hadn't been able to get in touch with her. Oh, but Jimmy, why did you run away? Where on earth did you think you could go?

It was a crisp cold night. Thank goodness it wasn't raining, Marcy muttered to herself as she ran down the gravel path to the parking lot. She reached a line of parked cars and started toward her Volkswagen when she was blinded by the headlights of an incoming car. She drew back to let it pass.

But the car didn't pass; instead, it pulled up short beside her. Marcy didn't hesitate. She turned quickly, running back the way she had come, moving faster when she heard someone get out of the car.

"Marcy!" It was Steve.

When she recognized his voice, she stopped and leaned against the hood of a car, panting. Still trembling, she watched him stride toward her.

"I didn't know it was you," she gasped. "I . . . I thought . . . you scared me."

"Well, good!" he bellowed. "You ought to be scared. What the hell are you doing out here by yourself this late at night?"

"I—it's this kid. I've got to pick him up."

"Now?"

"And I don't have much time. I've got to go."

"Not by yourself. Here, get in." He bundled her into his car, and Marcy didn't protest. She didn't have time to argue.

"Jake's Place," she told him. "It's a truck stop on Highway 80." While he drove, she told him about Jimmy. How unhappy he'd been since he was taken away from his alcoholic mother, when she'd disappeared for a week during one of her binges. How he'd been shuffled from home to home. How he didn't seem to fit in anywhere and had run away once before. "He's not a bad boy, and—well, I don't think the Emorys really understand him." Marcy felt close to tears as she thought about Jimmy. Maybe he, too, had been listening to Christmas music and been depressed by it. He'd probably heard other children making plans—family plans.

"I should have moved him, Steve. I knew he was unhappy there." Marcy's voice broke. She was suddenly overwhelmed by the sadness and the guilt. "He must have felt so alone."

Steve's hand covered hers. "No, Marcy, he was not alone. He called you, didn't he? From the truck stop?"

"Yes, but—"

"He knew you were there for him. He knew that you cared."

"Maybe," she said, sighing doubtfully. But the weight of guilt lifted just a little as the lights of the truck stop loomed ahead. Steve drove in and parked, then turned to her again.

"No maybe about it," he said. "When the chips are down and you're in trouble, real trouble, you call someone you can trust. He knew that. This Jimmy knew he could trust you." Steve rubbed the back of his hand gently against her cheek. "Come on, let's go see about the little scamp. Brave kid to walk out on a night like this. Foolish kid," he said as they went in.

The truck stop was typical. Warm and brightly lighted, filled with the smell of frying hamburgers and coffee. The trucker who had picked Jimmy up was a short stocky man with a genial face. He said he had kids of his own and didn't like to see any kid in trouble. And he sure didn't like to see them walking the highway, night *or* day. He had bought Jimmy a hamburger and hot chocolate. But now that they'd come for him, he said, he'd be on his way.

After thanking the trucker, Marcy slid into the booth beside Jimmy, whose frightened, tearstained face was raised to hers.

"Jimmy, why did you do this? And how? Didn't Mrs. Emory try to stop you?"

"I climbed out the window," Jimmy said, "after they went to sleep. And I don't want to go back there, Miss Wilson. They don't like me."

"Oh, Jimmy, why do you feel that way?" Marcy asked. Her mind was trying to grapple with the whole situation. Jimmy had to understand that he couldn't just run away like this, that it was wrong and he could get into trouble. But she had to try to find out what was wrong at the Emorys' and either straighten things out or else move him. She could tell he was frightened and anxious, and she was torn between the need to reprimand him, and her desire to comfort. "What makes you feel they don't like you?" she asked again.

"I just know. Please, Miss Wilson, don't make me go back. They don't like me."

"That doesn't matter." The calm voice was unexpected, and they both looked up to see Steve, who had appeared with two mugs of coffee. He gave one to Marcy, then sat across from them and looked intently at Jimmy. "You are going to meet lots of people, and some of them are not going to like you. The thing is, you have to like yourself. Do you like yourself, Jimmy?"

"Er...er...what do you mean?" Jimmy seemed puzzled, and perhaps, Marcy thought, a little intimidated by this man who was a stranger to him.

"Simple question. I asked you if you like yourself. Do you?"

Staring at Steve, the boy slowly nodded.

"Why?" Steve asked. "Why do you like yourself?"

"I...I play good soccer."

"Okay. That's fine for a start. What else do you like about yourself?"

Marcy sat spellbound as Steve drew Jimmy out, getting the boy to tell him in a faltering way that he was "pretty good at school," that he "didn't beat up on anybody" unless they picked on him first and that sometimes he ran errands for Mr. Orr, who was crippled.

"Well, you sound like a pretty good kid to me, Jimmy. Lots of reasons to like yourself. You're smart too, huh?"

Jimmy, more at ease now, nodded.

"Well then, tell me this," Steve said, taking a swallow of coffee, then setting down his mug. "How come a smart kid like you would do a dumb thing like this? Run away in the middle of the night and walk down a highway going nowhere?"

"I wasn't going nowhere. I was going to find my mama."

"You know where she is?"

"Well, no. But maybe I could find her." Jimmy bit his lip, his expression mutinous. "Anyway, I was mad 'cause Mrs. Emory took the money Miss Wilson gave me."

"Oh? Miss Wilson gave you some money?"

"For soccer shoes. 'Cause everybody on the team had soccer shoes but me. And I worked and made five dollars, but that wasn't enough, and Miss Wilson gave me the rest."

"And...?" Steve prompted, but his gaze had shifted to Marcy, and there was something in the way he looked at her that made the color steal into her cheeks. Embarrassed, she turned toward Jimmy, trying to concentrate on what he was saying.

He hadn't got the shoes at first because they didn't have his size. But Mrs. Emory had kept the money for him, and he was supposed to pick up the shoes yesterday. "Only—" here Jimmy looked rather sheepish "—me and Tad were fooling around on the way home from school. He had his soccer ball and we were kicking it back and forth, you know, and...well, it went right through Mr. Burton's window. He came out real mad and he said that windowpane was going to cost him fifteen dollars and somebody had to pay for it. Then Mrs. Emory came out and said I was responsible. And that wasn't fair!''

"It wasn't fair?" Steve's eyes were fixed on Jimmy. "Who kicked the ball?"

"I did," Jimmy admitted. "But...but...Tad missed it," he said defiantly. "If he'd just jumped up..."

"Wait a minute," Steve said. "It was you who kicked the ball that went through the window, right?"

"Right. But...but that money was for soccer shoes and Mrs. Emory shouldn't have given it to Mr. Burton." Jimmy gulped. Marcy could see that he was fighting back tears. "She kept saying I had to learn to be responsible."

"She's right, you know," Steve said. "You have to take the consequences for what you do. Even if what you did was an accident." He shrugged. "It's one of life's tougher lessons—and the sooner you learn it, the better."

But Marcy's heart went out to Jimmy. Poor little kid. Soccer shoes. First he'd got into a fight over them. Then when he finally had the money to buy them, it had to go for a broken windowpane. That was hard. But, of course, she knew that Mrs. Emory—and Steve—were right. Teaching the boy responsibility was more important than soccer shoes.

Mrs. Emory! Good Lord, if she missed him and reported... I'd better call, Marcy thought, and make some excuse. She glanced toward Jimmy, who was staring at Steve, completely absorbed in what he was saying. They hardly heard her when she told them she'd be back in a minute.

When she reached the public phone, she hesitated. What excuse could she possibly give Mrs. Emory? Calling her in the middle of the night and... She stopped. Jimmy had sneaked out of a window. Was there any chance they could sneak him back in? Oh, Marcy, what an unprofessional thing to do! Still...

When she returned to the booth she found Steve still talking confidentially to Jimmy, both of them eating apple pie and ice cream.

"Pie, Marcy?" Steve asked.

She shook her head.

"I was telling Steve that I want to find my mama," Jimmy explained. "She wouldn't treat me like Mrs. Emory, bossing me around and yelling at me all the time. My mama loves me."

"I don't know about that. She left you, didn't she?" Steve asked.

Oh, no! Marcy thought. That was cruel! Steve had gone too far. Jimmy was her case, and she shouldn't allow Steve to take over.

"Wait a minute, Steve," she started to say, but he broke in as if he knew what she was thinking.

"Miss Wilson doesn't think I should be talking to you," he said to Jimmy. "But I want to talk to you because when I was a little boy, I was just like you."

"You were?" Jimmy's eyes widened with astonishment.

"Exactly. My mother left me, too. Just walked out."

"She did? Was she sick?" Jimmy asked.

"No, she wasn't." Steve pushed away his half-finished pie, as if he had lost his appetite. "She just walked out." He sounded so sharp, so bitter, that Marcy's breath caught. For a moment, she felt confused. Diane had distinctly said that their mother died when Steve was five and Diane was two. Then she understood. When you were two you believed what you were told. But Steve, at five, had been old enough not to be fooled. Old enough to be hurt.

"How come?" Jimmy was asking. "How come your mama left you if she wasn't sick or anything?"

"I ... well, maybe in a way she was sick." Steve swallowed. "I ... I thought she would come back ... and I kept waiting...." Steve's voice broke, and there was such pain in his eyes that Marcy wanted to reach out, to comfort him.

"She didn't *never* come back?" Jimmy asked.

"No." For a long moment Steve was silent. Then he said, "So you see, I know how you feel. I felt all alone, too. My dad left me with people. And some of them—I could tell—didn't like me. You know?"

Jimmy's nod was full of understanding.

"Now," Steve said, "I know you're just ten years old."

"Ten years and two months," Jimmy said.

"Okay. And two months." Steve smiled. "Well, you'd better learn now that the main person you have to depend on is yourself. And you have to make the best of whatever situation you're in."

"But when people don't like you... Anyway, I bet nobody ever took your money."

"My father took all the money I earned one summer. My real father. And that's when *I* ran away from home."

While Jimmy exclaimed in a frenzy of empathy and anger, Diane's words came back to Marcy. *Steve was fifteen. He'd been caddying all summer at the golf course and was saving to buy a car. He gave me the money for that coat.... The very next day, he left home. Just walked out.* Steve's father had taken his car money! That was why he'd left home.

Oh, Steve, I'm so sorry!

"Later—much later—I knew why my father took that money," Steve said quietly. "He took it because he didn't make very much himself, and he had to pay most of that to the people who looked after us. It must have hurt his pride a great deal... but at the time, all I could see was that he'd taken *my* money. I was hurt and angry, and I decided to get out." He paused, staring down at the table, then looked directly into Jimmy's eyes. "I made the wrong decision.

"Maybe you want to run away because things aren't going the way you think they should," he continued. "But before you do, you ought to have somewhere to run. I was four years older than you, but just as dumb. I ran away with no place to go, no money, no education and no Miss Wilson to call.''

Marcy listened to Steve tell Jimmy of his precarious existence as a homeless teenager wandering from place to place. She knew that the episodes related were chosen deliberately and possibly exaggerated to scare the boy out of following the same course. But Marcy listened as avidly as Jimmy and was just as horrified. From the moment that Steve had walked into her office that September day, looking so confident and smiling that special smile, she had pictured him a strong, almost invincible man. Even when she had heard some of the details of his early life—how he couldn't get a job...lied about his age...joined the navy— she had thought him a man who did what needed to be done, no matter how difficult. Always confident, always in charge.

Now, as she watched him, and listened, his dark eyes serious and intent, full of compassion and determined to convince Jimmy of the dangers, she saw Steve in a different light. She saw a lonely, unhappy child, deserted by his mother—how could she have left him! She saw a frightened teenager, running, hiding to keep from being arrested as a vagrant.... Trapped in an alley by a gang of ruffians.... Always hungry, sleeping on the damp ground under a bridge, or, covered with a newspaper, huddled near the warm vent of a building. Marcy was as heartsick as Jimmy was frightened. She wanted to hold Steve in her arms, love him, make up for all he had been through. Yet she marveled at his wisdom and compassion and realized that what he had endured had helped to make him all that he was— strong and understanding. She was aware of the advice so cleverly woven in....

''Any home is better than none; don't expect it to be perfect.... Grown-ups have problems, too.... Lessons are important; I couldn't get a job because I didn't know anything.... Learn how to *do* something so you can earn money; folks always need windows washed or grass cut."

Marcy thought that if Jimmy was listening as intently as he appeared to be, sometimes forgetting his pie, he was learning lessons that could last him a lifetime. He seemed to have learned one lesson, anyway.

"Guess I'll stay at Mrs. Emory's, Miss Wilson. It ain't so bad. Nobody ever hits me, and she cooks good. And I did break that window."

So they took him back to the Emorys', where they managed to sneak him in through the same window he had climbed out of.

"Don't think of it as being unprofessional," Steve said, in answer to Marcy's qualms. "This comes under the heading of problem prevention."

"Why did you stop me from giving him the money for the soccer shoes?" she asked Steve, when she got back into the car.

"And reward him for running away?" Steve exclaimed, as he put the car in gear and headed home. "Besides, easy come, easy go."

"Oh, Steve, it's not as though he broke the window on purpose. And he wants those shoes so badly."

"That kid is on his own, Marcy. So he's got to learn to take care of himself. Handouts don't come easy. He's got to learn to work for what he wants, and learn to be responsible. It's rough out there."

Rough out there! That was what the trucker had said, too. Maybe, she thought, experience really was the best teacher. She had a degree in social work, but never could she have been as compellingly down-to-earth as Steve had been in his talk with Jimmy.

And never could she have been as compassionately honest. She looked at the man beside her, who had so exposed himself, who had dug up painful memories she knew he preferred to hide—to save a boy from making the same mistakes. She was so grateful to him for sharing his experience and his wisdom with Jimmy. But this feeling that filled her heart, flooded her whole being, was more than gratitude. It was a deep caring, something akin to adoration, for the Steve Prescott she had not known until tonight. Almost timidly she touched his arm.

"Steve, I want to thank you. It was very lucky that you came with me."

"Damn lucky!" He glanced at her, frowning a little. "It's not safe, Marcy—out by yourself this time of night. I'm glad I spotted you when I drove in from the airport."

"Oh! You're back from Connecticut." She couldn't help the twinge of pleasure she felt at the thought that he was home now. "Well, yes, I'm glad you came with me, of course. But I wasn't thinking of me."

"No, you never think of you. Some kid needs help and off you go whether it's storming or the middle of the night or—"

"Steve." She pressed his arm. "I want to tell you that what you did for Jimmy tonight was wonderful. Nobody could have talked to him the way you did. Could have made him understand so well."

"Maybe." He shrugged. "But lectures don't always do it. Guess some lessons have to be lived before you can learn 'em."

She was silent after that, thinking about lessons and life—and Steve. He was quiet, too. She realized it must have been a long day for him, and he was probably tired. Yet he had not hesitated to do what needed to be done.

When, finally, they'd walked up from the parking lot and stopped at her door, she turned toward him.

"Do you know what I think?" she said.

"No. What?" He smiled down at her.

"I think you are a very special person, Steve Prescott."
Standing on tiptoe, she kissed him, surprising him so that he
never let go of his bags. Then she went in, and shut the door.

WORK HAD PILED UP so that she didn't have a chance to visit
the Emorys until four days later. She hadn't seen Steve during those four days, either. Though she was exhausted, she'd
had Tom to dinner the next day, as promised. The day after
that, she had to attend a conference in Sacramento and
stayed overnight.

However, when she got home, the first thing she did was
call on Mrs. Emory.

"He seems to be doing better," Mrs. Emory said. "He's
not sassy like he used to be. And yesterday he asked me to
let him help wash windows. Can you believe that? Said he
wanted to learn how."

One night. One talk. Could it have made that much difference?

She spoke with Jimmy, too. Privately. Anxious to see if
he really wanted to remain with the Emorys.

"It's all right, I guess. Mr. Prescott says one place is
about as good as another."

"Mr. Prescott?"

"You know. That man that came with you when you
picked me up. He came to see me yesterday and gave me his
card. He told me to put it away real careful. His New York
office number is on there, and he says they always know
where he is and he's gonna tell them to always put me
through. So I can call him collect anytime. That is, whenever I really need to."

*He's got to learn to take care of himself, huh? You're a
softie, Steve.*

"He says I'm to write him. Let him know about my lessons. And when I finish high school, he says he'll help me
get a job. If I keep in touch. Maybe I can go to college."

When Marcy left, her heart was full. Steve's interest had extended far beyond one night. She had not known Steve was so...so good. He had accomplished more in one night than the welfare department had done in three years. Washing windows—"said he wanted to learn how." Learning to depend on himself. And Jimmy's face, Marcy thought, had lost that defeated "nobody likes me" look. He had made a friend, and his face was full of hope.

She thought of Steve. He was different from any man she had ever known. Gruff and callous on the outside. "I don't believe in this love-forever-after stuff." But so tender and caring on the inside. He was the best thing that could have happened to Diane's children. To Jimmy.

And to you, Marcy Wilson. You're a fool if you don't snap him up on any terms.

But marriage is different. I couldn't bear it if he didn't love me in a special way. She thought of Jennifer, her misery when Al had left. If I married Steve, and he left me or turned to another woman... "We'd both be free. We could go our separate ways."

No, she thought. I couldn't stand it. I couldn't bear it. It would hurt too much.

CHAPTER FOURTEEN

WHEN MARCY LEFT JIMMY, she went straight home. It was still a little early, but too late to go back to the office. These past three days had been difficult, and she knew she should feel tired.

But she didn't. She felt restless and strangely exhilarated, poised on tiptoe, waiting for something to happen.

Steve.

The kitten rolled at her feet, and she reached down and tickled his belly. After she'd filled his bowl with milk, she made herself a cup of tea. The tea, hot and spicy with chamomile, warmed and soothed her. She drank it slowly and thought about Steve.

Deliberately she made her mind dart away, fasten on her mother flying off to Japan. She'd received Marcy's gifts and was taking them with her. Good. Jennifer...Jennifer was happy, now. She and Al had left for their cruise this morning. Good. Jo...Marcy hadn't selected her gift yet. Maybe tomorrow at lunch.

Steve. What to think?

The kitten had not yet mastered the steps, so Marcy lifted him up and carried him to her loft. She kicked off her shoes, changed into jeans and a pullover. Then she lay across her bed and finally allowed herself to think about Steve Prescott.

"I don't believe in this love stuff." Just how important were the words "I love you" anyway? She was reminded of one of her father's favorite expressions, "What you do speaks so loudly I can't hear what you say."

Steve. He *said*, "I don't believe in love." Yet he exhibited more love than any man she knew. He had taken over the care of his sister's children so easily and naturally, acting out of love and not mere duty. And he had taken such a kindly, loving interest in Jimmy, a boy he hardly knew.

So he's a good guy. Nice to people. What does that mean to you?

It means he's a man worth loving.

And you love him?

Yes! Yes, I love him. The thought resounded almost defiantly as she looked down at the kitten, trying to get a good grip on a tennis ball that was too big for him to handle. She remembered another of her father's favorite sayings—the poet Browning's line, "A man's reach should exceed his grasp or what's a heaven for?"

Marriage, a real marriage, to Steve Prescott would be heaven. Dare she reach for it?

You're copping out, Marcy. A business marriage would be a mockery.

The kitten gave up on the tennis ball and clawed at the bed covers. Marcy scooped him up and put him on the bed beside her, where he purred contentedly as she stroked him.

Steve. I love him. I love everything about him. That crooked, engaging smile. I love his gruff way of taking charge. I love his cheerful teasing. I love the way he goes about doing whatever has to be done, whether it's changing a tire or scolding a runaway kid. I love his gentleness. The woman who marries him will be lucky.

She sat up, startling the kitten. He tumbled confusedly for a moment, then lay calmly down, placed one paw over the other and regarded her thoughtfully.

I could be that woman! He asked me to marry him. Me, Marcy Wilson. Nobody else.

Purely a business arrangement.

Maybe. But he does feel something for me. I know he does. The way he kissed me . . .

When he apologized for doing it? When he immediately backed away?

Because he was afraid! It came to her in a blinding flash of understanding. He was afraid to love, afraid he might be betrayed as he had once been betrayed by his mother. Again she saw the disillusionment in his face as clearly as she had seen it that night at the truck stop, when he had told Jimmy of his mother's desertion. Again she heard the bitterness in his voice that first night she had met him—*You can't trust women.* She had thought then that she'd misheard him. But she hadn't. That was truly how he felt. Because the woman he trusted most had betrayed him. Marcy knew well how the traumas of early childhood could hurt, could linger throughout life and affect one's whole outlook.

Steve's mother had left him. His father had taken his money. And the pain had cut so deep that he hid it, even from himself. But at the truck stop, in trying to break through to Jimmy, Steve had revealed his own hurt, his own fear. Strange, Marcy thought, that what happened to Steve had not made him unloving or unkind. Only afraid. To give love or receive it. To trust anyone.

She picked up the kitten, nestled her chin against his soft fur and tried to piece together the puzzle that was Steve Prescott. Strong. Dependable. Caring. Hurt. Confused. Untrusting. She longed to take him in her arms and love him so that he would never feel that kind of pain again. If she married him, she could teach him to love. To trust.

Almost subconsciously, she *visualized* it. Pictured being Steve's wife. Living with him. Each morning seeing that crooked smile across the breakfast table. Walking arm in arm with him under those great oak trees. Touching him, loving him. And being loved by him, his lips on hers, his hands caressing. Her imagination ran riot, and for moments she was gripped in an erotic fantasy of intense pleasure. Steve, holding her, loving her...

Reality intruded, punctured the dream. It couldn't be a real marriage. He might never love her, might never desire her as she desired him. He might fall in love with another woman.

But overriding the doubts and the dream loomed a very real possibility. If she didn't marry him, he would gradually disappear from her life. And there would be nothing left between them but the memory of what might have been. It was a grim prospect. No matter how, she had to be with him.

She would risk loving, rather than losing him.

Making the decision seemed to make her feel more alive. Happy. She wanted to run to Steve, to let him know she'd changed her mind, and now agreed to his crazy idea of a business marriage.

She smiled. Funny, it didn't seem crazy anymore. It seemed . . . well, right. She gave the kitten a gentle squeeze, set him on the floor and put on her loafers. Then she ran downstairs to Steve's apartment.

The woman who opened the door was beautiful, more beautiful even than her picture in the silver frame. *To my darling Steve, with all my love, Tricia.* The long wheat-colored hair was coiled in a loose knot and tied with a wide black ribbon. She had a perfect oval face, and hazel eyes that glinted with gold and slanted slightly. Her skin was flawless ivory above the low neck of her black cashmere sweater.

"Hello," she said, full red lips curving in that provocative smile. "Come in. You must be Marcy."

"Yes," admitted Marcy, smiling stiffly at the woman in black, as well as at Mrs. Chisholm, who had also come to the door. Mrs. Chisholm gave Marcy a knowing wink, and retreated to the kitchen. The *vision* repeated her invitation to come in.

She couldn't just walk away. Keenly aware of her old jeans and pullover and feeling a bit too short, Marcy followed the tall, graceful figure in the smart, black leather pants that seemed to be molded to her slender hips.

"Hi, Marcy! This is Tricia. Isn't she pretty?" Davey's eyes were big, his voice full of awe. Marcy resisted the impulse to shake him and agreed that, yes, Tricia was very pretty.

"Want some popcorn, Marcy?" Ginger asked.

"Yes, do have some. And join us." Tricia, the beautiful, gestured to a big bowl of popcorn and sank gracefully to the floor beside it. The glow from the fire and the lights of the Christmas tree enhanced her exquisite features and made a halo around her wheat-colored hair. She looked not only gorgeous, but very much at home. And Marcy wanted to dump the bowl of popcorn over her head. And I probably would, she thought, if I stayed another minute!

"No thanks," she managed to say. "I'll just be on my way and—"

"Eat some, Marcy. It's real good." Ginger tugged at her hand, pulling her to the floor. Marcy took a few kernels and choked them down while Ginger watched.

"Don't you like it? Didn't Tricia make it good?"

"Yes, she did," said Marcy. Big deal! What's to do with corn but pop it?

"Marcy, look what Trish brought us! It's a puzzle from the New York zoo. It's got lots of animals." Davey carefully placed a piece in the giant jigsaw puzzle. "I think this one goes right here, don't you, Tricia?"

"How nice," said Marcy. She wondered where Steve was but didn't want to ask. It was bad enough watching this cozy threesome. She felt isolated, out of place.

"Well, I must be going," she said again.

"No, wait," Tricia urged. "Steve went on an errand, but he'll be right back. Did you want to see him about something?"

"Well, I . . . it . . . it's nothing important."

"Why don't you wait? Here, let me get you a glass of wine."

"No," Marcy said quickly and firmly, feeling a flash of irritation at the way this woman was taking charge—as if she, Tricia, were mistress of the place. Offering her wine. Steve's wine! What gave her the right?

Marcy felt suddenly ashamed. What was the matter with her? She had never in all her life taken such an instant dislike to anyone. She made herself smile, made her voice congenial.

"It's nice to finally meet you, Tricia. Are you enjoying your stay?" *How long will you be here? Don't ask!*

"Oh, yes, I'm enjoying myself very much."

"We're going to 'neticut," Ginger said excitedly. "And Tricia's coming, too."

Marcy felt a stabbing pain of apprehension.

"And we're going to have ponies," Davey added, looking up from his puzzle. "And Tricia's going to teach us to ride. Aren't you, Tricia?"

The apprehension turned to despair. Steve had hired his wife! Tricia. Tricia would be there. Living with Steve, with the children. Marcy wanted to stand up and run out of the apartment, but her knees felt weak and she couldn't move. She just sat there, all the will gone out of her.

Ginger said she was going to name her pony Bozo. And Davey said that wasn't any kind of a name for a horse, was it, Tricia? He was going to name his pony King or Captain. Tricia asked if Marcy had seen pictures of the Connecticut place, and she took the photographs from the coffee table and began to talk about them. She said she thought the stable should be enlarged, and if it was, then the paddock could be placed here. She pointed a slender finger.

They all seemed to be talking at once, and the words flowed around Marcy, confused and sounding far away. She kept saying "yes" and "no" and "how nice," and she couldn't find the strength to stand up, to run. Finally, she did manage to pull herself to her feet.

"I must go," she said. "I have to...to buy some cat food."

"Oh, I'm sorry," said the vision. "Steve did say he'd be right back but... Could I give him a message?"

"No. No. It's not important." And all the way out of the door and back to her apartment, she kept telling herself that it really wasn't important. It didn't matter. It was best this way.

She sat on her sofa, staring at the ashes in the cold fireplace. She felt as though she were drowning. As though she were floundering in a dark empty sea, and there was nothing, no one, to hold on to.

Steve.

She told herself she was lucky. Lucky to have seen Tricia first. Before she'd had a chance to run to Steve and babble her heart out.

Oh, Steve! How could you!

You are a fool, Marcy. You thought . . . *He asked me to marry him. Me, Marcy Wilson. Nobody else.* But she had refused, so he asked Tricia.

A thought struck her.

Maybe he'd asked Tricia first, and *she* had refused! Of course. They had been friends . . . lovers? . . . long before he ever met Marcy. And now Tricia had changed her mind and accepted him. And probably not for hire. For real! She would be Steve's wife—living with him and loving him. Marcy turned her head against the sofa pillow, trying to block out the thought. The desolation.

Again she told herself she was lucky. It couldn't have worked out. She couldn't have been happy with Steve. Loving him, and not being loved in return.

But she wasn't happy now. Without Steve, there was a crying, aching emptiness. She couldn't bear it. She couldn't.

Marcy lifted her head. Jennifer. She was acting just like Jennifer. Dependent. Desolate. Unhappy.

Well, she wasn't going to live that way! She would be perfectly happy without him. Marcy Wilson's life did not revolve around Steve Prescott.

The cat pulled at her pant leg, and she reached down to pick him up. Cat food. She had to buy some cat food. Wearily she got up, plugged in the tree lights and watched the tiny beams appear against the white flocking and the golden bells.

Christmas. A happy time. Jennifer would be away with Al, her mother with Bill and his family in Japan. Maybe, Marcy decided, she'd fix Christmas dinner for Gerald and his father. No. She might go to the cabin with Jo and her family. She would think happy. And be happy. After all, she had good friends, a good job, a lovely apartment....

The phone rang. She put down the kitten to answer it.

Tom. At first she said no, she was just too tired.

"Please," he said. He had to talk to her.

So she said yes, he could come over for a little while.

STEVE PUT DOWN his coffee cup and smiled at Trish. He thought it must be almost time for her friends to pick her up. He liked Trish, and when she'd called, saying that she was in San Francisco for a modeling job and that some friends were driving up to visit relatives in Auburn, he'd told her sure, come along, he'd like to have her come and visit. But now... He wouldn't look at his watch.

"That was a delicious dinner, Steve."

"Yes, Mrs. Chisholm is an excellent cook." Wasn't it six yet? They had said they'd be back about six. Marcy. She had the darnedest way of disappearing. He hadn't seen her for several days, and he needed to talk to her.

"Will you be taking her with you when you move?"

"I sure hope so. I..." He stopped. Tricia was speaking of Mrs. Chisholm. "Well, that is, I'd like to," he hastily amended, "but she has a family here." Mrs. Chisholm would be through bathing the kids soon, and then she'd be off. But he desperately wanted her to stay, and Trish to leave, so he could go over to Marcy's.

Trish snubbed out her cigarette and poured herself another cup of coffee.

"More coffee, Steve?"

"No. No, thank you." He realized he wasn't being a good host, so he remarked very heartily that her career certainly seemed to be taking off.

"Yes," she said. "I have a shoot in Paris next month." She talked about her modeling jobs for a while, then began to fill him in on what all their friends in New York were doing. He listened with half an ear, his mind on his own problems. He had finally made an offer on that place in Connecticut, and now was wondering whether he'd done the right thing. He hadn't had time to check on schools. He wasn't even sure that Marcy had really liked the place. She'd been so reticent that night he'd shown her the pictures. He wanted to talk with her anyway. He wanted to see her. Darn it! Sometimes she could be so evasive. Abruptly he stood, motioning for Trish to accompany him to the living room. He tossed another log on the fire, and dusted his hands. Tricia came up behind him and slowly, sensuously, began to massage his shoulders.

"Oh! Did Mrs. Chisholm tell you? The little social worker from next door stopped by."

"Marcy?" Steve moved out of Tricia's reach, and turned to face her. "What did she want?"

Tricia shrugged. "She said it was nothing important. But I have my own ideas."

"What's that supposed to mean?"

Tricia moved close to him and trailed her fingers along his jawline. "She's just like the rest of us. Charmed beyond our good sense by a man named Stephen Prescott."

"You're wrong about that. She's given me no reason to think I'm charming. And Marcy's not like anyone I've ever known."

"Oh?" Tricia raised an eyebrow. "Would you care to elaborate?"

"Well, she's . . . very . . . very officious." He fumbled for more benign words, not wanting to share with Trish all that Marcy was. "Unselfish. A truly dedicated social worker." The doorbell rang. Thank God, Trish's friends were here!

They didn't stay long, and he rejoiced when he finally closed the door behind them. Tricia had hinted that he might drive her down to San Francisco, spend a few days there. Steve turned down her invitation, and she did not persist. They parted, as always, uncommitted.

He asked Mrs. Chisholm to remain at the apartment while he went on an errand. She agreed, reminding him to pick up some milk for the children's morning cereal.

Steve went out, but just as he started toward Marcy's door, he saw her walking down the steps with Horn Rims. They didn't see him, and he watched them walk on toward the parking lot. The guy's arm was entwined around Marcy's waist. She was laughing and looking up at him in a way that made Steve's temples pound. His pulse raced and there was a peculiar feeling in the pit of his stomach.

Jealous, old buddy?

Hell, no! It was just that every time he needed Marcy, she was unavailable. And he was getting pretty sick of these guys always hanging around her. When we get married . . .

If you get married.

For a moment he was seized by a feeling of near-panic. Then it was replaced by a spurt of angry determination.

Not if! When. I will convince her and I don't care how long it takes. No way will I go off to New York and leave Marcy here.

Horn Rims. The nerve of that guy! Holding on to Marcy as if he owned her!

Steve realized that he was standing with his hands thrust in his pockets, staring after the two people who had already disappeared. He turned to go back to his apartment, then remembered Mrs. Chisholm's request for milk and turned again to walk toward his car.

He felt restless, ill at ease, and . . . well, abandoned. He told himself that was crazy. Just because he hadn't been in touch with Marcy for a couple of days, and she had a date tonight . . . Well, damn it, he needed to talk with her. He wanted to get things settled! He slammed the door of his car, shoved it into gear and drove out of the lot with an unusual burst of speed.

The way Marcy had looked up at Horn Rims... *I'm not in love with anyone,* she had declared when Steve asked her point-blank. But she sure could give a guy the wrong impression. Marcy was too trusting... and too giving, and people could take advantage of her.

Friendship, she called it. Good old-fashioned friendship. That was what she'd said about Gerald. Gerald, who had a key to her place and slept over at his convenience! I bet there's more than friendship on his mind!

Steve was only dimly aware that he had passed the cutoff to the supermarket, and that his speedometer was creeping toward seventy, until he heard the siren and saw the flashing light.

"Going to a fire, buddy?" asked the good-natured patrolman who gave him the ticket.

"More like a funeral." Steve sighed, unable to rid himself of the feeling of abandonment. He pulled back onto the highway at a more moderate speed, now feeling more emptiness than anger. The lights of Jake's Place loomed ahead and, without knowing why, he turned into the parking lot.

Inside, the waitress asked if he wanted anything besides coffee. He said no, and sat there in the booth, the same booth he had shared with Marcy and Jimmy. He tried to recapture the slightest fragment of all that he had felt that night. They had been so close, he and Marcy. So in unison. Together. And later, when he had stood at her door, the way she'd looked into his eyes and stood on tiptoe to kiss him.

You are a very special person, Steve Prescott.

Even now he remembered the warmth of that moment. The sense of belonging that he had never known before. The love that had shone in Marcy's eyes. *Love for him.* And she had said she believed in that love-forever-after stuff....

Steve Prescott, you're a fool! You don't want to *talk* to Marcy. You want to hold her in your arms, kiss her until she's breathless, be with her forever.

Hire a wife! Who are you kidding? You love Marcy like crazy and you're afraid to admit it to yourself. You want the whole thing—love...honor...cherish...cleave to me only. Yes, damn it! No Geralds. No Horn Rims. And no Tricias, either.

I've got to see her. I've got to tell her. Steve tucked a dollar bill under the saucer and hurried out.

MARCY PLACED a half-dozen cans of cat food in the grocery cart.

She was very fond of Tom and never wanted to cause him pain. But she couldn't love him the way he deserved to be loved. She couldn't lead him on, allow him to hope. It would be unfair.

And so she had turned down his proposal, turned down his plea to think things over and join his family in Sausalito for Christmas.

Christmas.

"Excuse me, please."

"Oh, I'm sorry." Marcy realized her cart was blocking the aisle and pushed it out of the way. What would Christmas be like this year? Without Steve or the children. Without her dreams.

But she had to stop dreaming and go on living! Dinner. She hadn't eaten. But she really wasn't hungry. Still, her mother's voice echoed in her thoughts..."Have something warm, and you'll feel better." The fresh oysters in the fish section ahead caught her eye and she reached for them, almost smelling the aroma of homemade stew.

WHY IS THE MILK always at the back of the store? Steve grumbled as he threaded his way through the aisles. Why do things that seem so right go wrong? Why was Marcy with Horn Rims when she ought to be with him? *He could never love her as I do.* No one could.

I love her! And she loves me, too. I know it.

He did truly love Marcy in a way he had never thought possible. And she didn't know, because he had never told her.

Damn it! He would tell her. He'd make her understand.

MARCY'S HAND HOVERED over the jars of oysters. Three ninety-five each! She'd have to put back some of the cat food in order to pay....

"Marcy, I've got to tell you something. Put that down!"

The voice had boomed out of nowhere, and automatically, Marcy answered. "I am. I'm going to put back some of the—" Marcy spun around in sudden realization. "Steve!"

"Did you hear what I said? I've got to tell you something."

"I don't want to hear it!" Marcy became conscious of a woman watching them and lowered her voice. "There's no need to tell me." She didn't want him to tell her. She couldn't bear to hear him say, "I'm marrying Trish."

Steve looked at her in surprise. "Marcy, you have to listen to me. You have to know—"

"You don't need to tell me. I already know."

"You know? How could you when I didn't know myself?"

"The children told me." She bit her lip. "And I'm very happy for you." She turned her head away. Dear Lord, don't let me cry now.

"The children told you what? Wait a minute." He shoved Marcy's cart aside. A woman standing nearby clapped her hand over her mouth and scurried away. "I'm trying to tell you I love you and you keep babbling about something the children said."

She wasn't sure what she'd just heard. She took a few steps back to look up at him. Her shoulder brushed against a pile of cans stacked for display and they came crashing down. Several people turned to look.

"Oh, hell." Steve got on his knees and began to restack the cans.

Marcy sank down on her knees beside him. "Steve, what did you say?"

"You keep babbling something about the children."

"No, before that. Did you say you love...?"

"Yes, I love you, Marcy. And I want you to marry me. To really be my wife."

"But I thought...Tricia..." She stopped. What did Tricia matter now?

Steve was holding a can of tomatoes and he was looking into her eyes, telling her that he loved her, and those were the sweetest words she had ever heard him say. She was laughing...and she was crying...and she felt giddy and excited...and wonderful. She moved closer, cupped his face in her hands and kissed him.

"Lady, this don't look like no fight to me."

They glanced up to see the woman and two strong clerks grinning down at them just as the store lights dimmed.

"Never mind about those cans, folks," one of the clerks said. "We'll take care of them."

Marcy hardly heard. She could only gaze into Steve's eyes and see that her dreams were coming true.

Steve stood and clasped her hand, pulling her to her feet, and into his arms. He held her close. As she felt his lips on hers, waves of exaltation and happiness flooded through her. Her heart sang in joyous rhythm with the Christmas music that echoed through the store.

The crowd around them applauded.

"Come on, folks," a clerk pleaded. "Time to go. It's the end of the day."

Steve and Marcy smiled at the people around them and walked out, arm in arm, knowing it was the beginning of a lifetime.

ATTRACTIVE, SPACE SAVING BOOK RACK

Display your most prized novels on this handsome and sturdy book rack. The hand-rubbed walnut finish will blend into your library decor with quiet elegance, providing a practical organizer for your favorite hard-or soft-covered books.

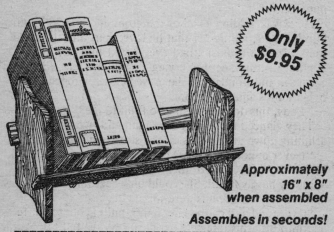

Only $9.95

Approximately 16" x 8" when assembled

Assembles in seconds!

To order, rush your name, address and zip code, along with a check or money order for $10.70* ($9.95 plus 75¢ postage and handling) payable to *Harlequin Reader Service*:

Harlequin Reader Service
Book Rack Offer
901 Fuhrmann Blvd.
P.O. Box 1396
Buffalo, NY 14269-1396

Offer not available in Canada.

BKR-1A

*New York and Iowa residents add appropriate sales tax.

Harlequin Intrigue
Adopts a New Cover Story!

**We are proud to present to you
the new Harlequin Intrigue cover design.**

Look for two exciting new stories each month, which mix a contemporary, sophisticated romance with the surprising twists and turns of a puzzler . . . romance with "something more."

INTNC-R

HARLEQUIN SIGNATURE EDITION

CAROLE MORTIMER

JUST ONE NIGHT

Hawk Sinclair—Texas millionaire and owner of the exclusive
Sinclair hotels, determined to protect his son's inheritance.
Leonie Spencer—desperate to protect her sister's happiness.

They were together for just one night.
The night their daughter was conceived.

Blackmail, kidnapping and attempted murder add suspense
to passion in this exciting bestseller.

The success story of Carole Mortimer continues with *Just
One Night*, a captivating romance from the author of the
bestselling novels, *Gypsy* and *Merlyn's Magic*.

**Available in March
wherever paperbacks are sold.**

WTCH-1